YAS

**FRIENDS
OF ACPL**

Jay-Z

Other books in the People in the News series:

Maya Angelou
David Beckham
Beyoncé
Fidel Castro
Kelly Clarkson
Hillary Clinton
Miley Cyrus
Hilary Duff
Zac Efron
Brett Favre
50 Cent
Al Gore
Tony Hawk
Salma Hayek
LeBron James
Derek Jeter
Dwayne Johnson
Angelina Jolie
Coretta Scott King
Ashton Kutcher
Tobey Maguire
John McCain
Barack Obama
Nancy Pelosi
Queen Latifah
Daniel Radcliffe
Condoleezza Rice
Rihanna
J.K. Rowling
Shakira
Tupac Shakur
Will Smith
Gwen Stefani
Ben Stiller
Hilary Swank
Justin Timberlake
Usher
Oprah Winfrey

Jay-Z

by Laurie Collier Hillstrom

LUCENT BOOKS
A part of Gale, Cengage Learning

Detroit • New York • San Francisco • New Haven, Conn • Waterville, Maine • London

© 2010 Gale, Cengage Learning

ALL RIGHTS RESERVED. No part of this work covered by the copyright herein may be reproduced, transmitted, stored, or used in any form or by any means graphic, electronic, or mechanical, including but not limited to photocopying, recording, scanning, digitizing, taping, Web distribution, information networks, or information storage and retrieval systems, except as permitted under Section 107 or 108 of the 1976 United States Copyright Act, without the prior written permission of the publisher.

Every effort has been made to trace the owners of copyrighted material.

LIBRARY OF CONGRESS CATALOGING-IN-PUBLICATION DATA

Hillstrom, Laurie Collier, 1965-
  Jay-Z / by Laurie Collier Hillstrom.
    p. cm.— (People in the news)
  Includes bibliographical references and index.
  ISBN 978-1-4205-0158-2 (hardcover)
  1. Jay-Z, 1969—Juvenile literature. 2. Rap musicians—United States—Biography—Juvenile literature. I. Title.
   ML3930.J38H55 2010
   782.421649092—dc22
   [B]
                                                                2009031523

Lucent Books
27500 Drake Rd
Farmington Hills, MI 48331

ISBN 13: 978-1-4205-0158-2
ISBN 10: 1-4205-0158-5

Printed in the United States of America
1 2 3 4 5 6 7 13 12 11 10 09

Printed by Bang Printing, Brainerd, MN, 1st Ptg., 11/2009

Contents

Foreword	6
Introduction	8
Rising from the Lobby to the Penthouse	
Chapter 1	11
Growing Up in the Ghetto	
Chapter 2	25
Hitting It Big in Rap Music	
Chapter 3	41
Retiring as a Rap Artist	
Chapter 4	54
Becoming a Business Mogul	
Chapter 5	65
Having It All	
Notes	81
Important Dates	86
For More Information	88
Index	90
Picture Credits	95
About the Author	96

Foreword

Fame and celebrity are alluring. People are drawn to those who walk in fame's spotlight, whether they are known for great accomplishments or for notorious deeds. The lives of the famous pique public interest and attract attention, perhaps because their experiences seem in some ways so different from, yet in other ways so similar to, our own.

Newspapers, magazines, and television regularly capitalize on this fascination with celebrity by running profiles of famous people. For example, television programs such as *Entertainment Tonight* devote all their programming to stories about entertainment and entertainers. Magazines such as *People* fill their pages with stories of the private lives of famous people. Even newspapers, newsmagazines, and television news frequently delve into the lives of well-known personalities. Despite the number of articles and programs, few provide more than a superficial glimpse at their subjects.

Lucent's People in the News series offers young readers a deeper look into the lives of today's newsmakers, the influences that have shaped them, and the impact they have had in their fields of endeavor and on other people's lives. The subjects of the series hail from many disciplines and walks of life. They include authors, musicians, athletes, political leaders, entertainers, entrepreneurs, and others who have made a mark on modern life and who, in many cases, will continue to do so for years to come.

These biographies are more than factual chronicles. Each book emphasizes the contributions, accomplishments, or deeds that have brought fame or notoriety to the individual and shows how that person has influenced modern life. Authors portray their subjects in a realistic, unsentimental light. For example, Bill Gates—the cofounder and chief executive officer of the software giant Microsoft—has been instrumental in making personal computers the most vital tool of the modern age. Few dispute his business savvy, his perseverance, or his technical expertise, yet critics say he is ruthless in his dealings with competitors and driven more by his desire to maintain Microsoft's dominance in the computer industry than by an interest in furthering technology.

In these books, young readers will encounter inspiring stories about real people who achieved success despite enormous obstacles. Oprah Winfrey—the most powerful, most watched, and wealthiest woman on television today—spent the first six years of her life in the care of her grandparents while her unwed mother sought work and a better life elsewhere. Her adolescence was colored by promiscuity, pregnancy at age fourteen, rape, and sexual abuse.

Each author documents and supports his or her work with an array of primary and secondary source quotations taken from diaries, letters, speeches, and interviews. All quotes are footnoted to show readers exactly how and where biographers derive their information and provide guidance for further research. The quotations enliven the text by giving readers eyewitness views of the life and accomplishments of each person covered in the People in the News series.

In addition, each book in the series includes photographs, annotated bibliographies, timelines, and comprehensive indexes. For both the casual reader and the student researcher, the People in the News series offers insight into the lives of today's newsmakers—people who shape the way we live, work, and play in the modern age.

Introduction

Rising from the Lobby to the Penthouse

Jay-Z is widely considered to be the most successful rap artist of all time. He has sold more than thirty million records, dominated radio airplay, and won several Grammy Awards during the course of his career. "He spit cool and witty with devastating flows, dropped classic albums, influenced MCs, changed pop culture, and built a tall stack of dollars in the process," noted a writer for *Rolling Stone*. "We've witnessed not merely a Hall of Fame career but one of the top-shelf greatest of all time."[1]

Yet Jay-Z's legacy extends far beyond the music he has created. He also built his own business empire—including an influential record label and a popular clothing line—and ascended to one of the most powerful positions in the music industry as president and CEO of Def Jam Records. His rise to the top is all the more remarkable considering where he started. "I've taken the whole ride," Jay-Z acknowledged. "I didn't skip any floors. I started at the lower lobby. Went all the way up to the penthouse."[2]

Jay-Z grew up poor in a tough New York City neighborhood. After being abandoned by his father, he became a teenaged drug dealer. Yet Jay-Z eventually escaped the dead-end life of a street hustler through talent, determination, and ambition. He stands as an example "of what anyone—no matter their class, economic level, race, environment, social status, or adversities—can achieve with hard work and hustle," Jake Brown wrote in *Jay-Z…and the Roc-A-Fella Records Dynasty*. "Jay-Z is a fundamental example of the hip-hop renaissance man, and a

Jay-Z is considered by many to be the most successful rap artist of all time.

pioneer of the model—street hustler to rap star to rap mogul in his own right."³

By combining musical talent, business acumen, and street smarts, Jay-Z has emerged as one of the most influential figures in American music and hip-hop culture. His success story serves as an inspiration to his many fans. "Jay-Z's trailblazing contributions to hip-hop culture across America and throughout the world have helped raise the aspirations of millions of people," Def Jam Records co-founder Russell Simmons wrote. "He has had the courage to tell vivid stories about the realities of the urban experience with the precision of a master therapist whose words and rhymes tap into the consciousness of people who yearn for a better life.... Today Jay-Z stands center stage with the penetrating sustainability of a living legend."[4]

Chapter 1

Growing Up in the Ghetto

Part of Jay-Z's enormous appeal in the world of hip-hop comes from his "street cred." When he raps about poverty, crime, drugs, and violence, he speaks from experience. Jay-Z grew up in a tough urban neighborhood and got a firsthand look at life as a drug dealer. But he used music to lift himself out of this cruel and self-destructive existence. His remarkable rise from the streets of the ghetto to the top of the recording industry helped him earn the respect and admiration of millions of fans.

Grows Up in the Marcy Projects

Jay-Z was born on December 4, 1969, in Brooklyn, one of the five boroughs that make up New York City. His real name is Shawn Corey Carter. His mother, Gloria Carter, worked as an investment clerk. His father, Adnes (some sources say Adnis) Reeves, held a series of odd jobs. "My pops did anything from cabdriver to truck driver to working at the phone company,"[5] Jay-Z recalled. Shawn was the youngest of four children in his family. He had one older brother, Eric, and two older sisters, Andrea (known as Annie) and Michelle (known as Mickey).

Shawn grew up in the Marcy Projects, a large public-housing complex for low-income families, located in the Bedford-Stuyvesant neighborhood of Brooklyn. Built in 1949, Marcy consisted of 27 six-story apartment buildings that housed

A view of the Brooklyn borough of New York where Jay-Z grew up.

more than 4,000 people. It was a tough place to grow up, full of drugs, crime, and hopelessness. In fact, CBS News once described the Marcy complex as "among the most dangerous places in America."[6] Looking back, though, Jay-Z noted that his background gave him a valuable perspective on life:

> I wouldn't want to grow up no other way. It shaped me, taught me integrity.... You've got kids that inherited stuff from their parents [and] they don't appreciate it because it was no work; there's no A to Z, it's just Z. To me, you need somewhere to start, somewhere to be like, "Man, I ain't never going back to not being able to pay my light bill, my stomach growling, eating cereal at night, peanut butter and jelly off the spoon, mayonnaise sandwiches." This is real.[7]

Despite the hardships that he suffered, Shawn managed to keep a positive attitude. Even as a boy, he was a bit of a showoff and enjoyed being the center of attention. His friends and neighbors

The Famous Faces of Bed-Stuy

The Bedford-Stuyvesent (Bed-Stuy) neighborhood of Brooklyn where Jay-Z grew up is famous for producing a number of well-known African-American musicians, actors, and athletes. It was the childhood home of such hip-hop and rhythm-and-blues (R&B) stars as Aaliyah, Busta Rhymes, Fabolous, Lil' Kim, Mos Def, and the Notorious B.I.G. Professional basketball player and coach Lenny Wilkens grew up in Bed-Stuy, as did boxer Mike Tyson. Comedian Chris Rock spent his youth there, then turned the neighborhood into the setting for his autobiographical TV series *Everybody Hates Chris*. Bed-Stuy also was featured prominently in comedian Dave Chappelle's documentary film *Block Party* and in a number of movies directed by Brooklyn native Spike Lee.

gave him the nickname "Jazzy," which he eventually shortened to create his stage name, Jay-Z. "When I was young, I had the same demeanor as I do now. I was a cool kid, a jazzy little dude. People would say, 'Yo, it's Jazzy!'" he explained. "I liked the way it flowed so I took the Jay and the Z."[8]

Learns to Love Music

Even as a boy, Shawn loved music. His parents had twelve crates full of record albums that they had collected over the years. Each album had a label with the owner's name on it, and no one else in the family was allowed to touch it without permission. "These people shared everything," Jay-Z remembered about his parents, "but not those records. It was like, 'This is my son and your son. This is my house and your house. But this is my record.' That's just to show you how much they loved their music."[9]

Gloria Carter always listened to music on Saturdays while she cleaned the family's apartment. Even when he was outdoors, Shawn could hear his mother's soul and funk records blaring through the open windows. He loved the rhythm of the music, but he often found himself making up different words to match the beat. He spent hours at the kitchen table playing with words, coming up with inventive rhymes, and experimenting with song lyrics. "I had this green notebook that I used to write in incessantly," he recalled. "I would walk through the Marcy projects, where everyone's playing basketball, with my notebook, and that was not a cool thing."[10]

If Shawn did not have his notebook handy, he wrote down lyrics on scraps of paper or grocery sacks and stuffed them into his pockets. When all these scraps of paper became annoying, Shawn developed the ability to compose entire songs in his head without writing them down. "I started running around in the streets, and that's how not writing came about," he explained. "I was comin' up with these ideas, and I'd write 'em on a paper bag, and I had all these paper bags in my pocket, and I hate a lot of things in my pocket, so I started memorizing and holding it."[11]

Abandoned by His Father

As Shawn approached his teen years, he dreamed of making a career in music. He needed this dream to sustain him when his family was suddenly torn apart. In 1981, when Shawn was eleven, his father left home. Adnes Reeves divorced his wife and had no further contact with his children. Shawn was devastated. "Kids look up to they pop like Superman. Superman just left the crib? That's traumatic," he acknowledged. "He was a good guy. It's just that he didn't handle the situation well. He handled it so bad that you forgot all the good he did."[12]

Shawn struggled to deal with feelings of pain, anger, confusion, and resentment after his father left the family. He developed a fear of abandonment that made it difficult for him to establish close relationships with other people. "I changed a lot. I became more guarded," he said. "I never wanted to be attached to something and get that taken away again. I never wanted to feel that feeling again."[13]

When Jay-Z was eleven, he got a gun and shot his older brother when Eric stole from him.

Shawn's mother worried about him and did her best to keep him out of trouble. She bought him his own boom box to encourage his interest in music. Despite her best efforts, though, the family went through some tough times. Money was tight, and they often struggled to pay the electric bill or put food on the table. Shawn's brother, Eric, started doing drugs and became addicted. One day, when Shawn was twelve, he caught Eric stealing a ring that belonged to him. Eric planned to sell the ring for money to buy drugs. Angry and disappointed, Shawn got a gun from someone on the street and shot his older brother in the shoulder. Luckily, Eric recovered from the wound and forgave him, and Shawn did not face criminal charges.

Becomes a Teenaged Drug Dealer

As he watched his family struggle in the absence of his father, Shawn found it hard to resist the temptations he saw around him on the street. Many people in the projects, like his

Jay-Z needed money and sold crack cocaine in Brooklyn and New Jersey during his youth.

brother, turned to drugs as a way to escape from their problems. Other people—including kids his own age—made lots of money by selling drugs. The drug of choice in his neighborhood at that time was crack cocaine. It was very popular among poor drug users because it was cheaper than regular cocaine but produced an intense high. Crack use spread through large American cities like an epidemic in the mid-1980s, contributing to existing problems like homelessness, poverty, and crime. The crack epidemic hit the Marcy Projects hard. "It was a plague in that neighborhood," Jay-Z remembered. "It was just everywhere, everywhere you look. In the hallways. You could smell it in the hallways."[14]

In the midst of the crack epidemic, Shawn felt that he had two choices: do drugs or sell drugs. "It was either you're doin' it or you was movin' it,"[15] he stated. After witnessing the effects of his brother's addiction, Shawn was determined not to do drugs. But the lure of easy money was very powerful, so he started working as a drug dealer. He sold crack cocaine in his Brooklyn neighborhood, then gradually expanded his territory into New Jersey. The money he earned enabled him to buy nice clothes and

A Solid Student

Before he dropped out of high school to pursue a career in music, Jay-Z was a very good student. By the time he reached sixth grade, he was already reading at a twelfth-grade level. In addition, his remarkable memory—which he used to compose entire songs in his head—helped him perform well on tests.

Jay-Z's favorite teacher was Renee Rosenblum-Lowden, who taught his English class in middle school. "She took our class to her house in Brooklyn on a field trip," he recalled. "You know how many teachers would take a bunch of black kids to their house?" His teacher remembered him as a sweet, good-natured young man with a gift for language. "He was a very dear kid," Rosenblum-Lowden said. "There is so much more to him than a [stereotypical rapper]. Gee, I hope I'm not killing his image."

Sources: Quoted in "Celebrities Remember Their Teachers," *Instructor*, August 2004, p. 9; Quoted in Nick Charles and Cynthia Wang, "Street Singer: Jay-Z Makes the Switch from Hustler to Rap Star Look E-Z," *People Weekly*, April 5, 1999, p. 61.

---

jewelry. He also gave some to his mother to help his family live more comfortably.

Although he needed the money, Shawn knew that selling illegal drugs exposed him to a great deal of risk. He had to watch his back all the time to avoid getting caught by the police. He felt nervous anytime he saw a police car in his rearview mirror. He also had to be careful to avoid confrontations with other drug dealers. He knew that many people in his line of work became victims of violence. For these reasons, Shawn never considered drug dealing to be a long-term career choice. "I knew I had to get out because the only future is jail or die," he noted. "I wasn't locked up, I didn't see a friend killed, no tragedy; it was more like mortality and fear. You get wiser, and the years go by, and you're not moving anywhere. I've seen this story play out a million times."[16]

Starts Rapping

Even as he continued to hustle drugs on the street, Shawn also worked toward building a brighter future for himself. He went to school and got good grades. He attended Eli Whitney High School in his neighborhood until it closed down, then qualified for admission to Brooklyn's prestigious George Westinghouse Technical High School. It was there that he met several fellow students who shared his interest in music, including Christopher Wallace (who later became known as the Notorious B.I.G. or Biggie Smalls).

Shawn and his friends were intrigued by hip-hop, a relatively new form of music that gained widespread popularity in the mid-1980s. Hip-hop originated in New York City during the 1970s, when a Jamaican DJ named Kool Herc began reciting his own rhymes over the background beat of recorded music. Before long, kids throughout the city were going to house parties where DJs used multiple turntables to mix parts of popular records together to create new songs. Talented MCs rapped rhyming lyrics to the music, while people in the crowd performed break-dancing moves. By the middle of the 1980s, hip-hop songs by groups like Run DMC and the Beastie Boys had started to receive some radio airplay.

Shawn practiced rapping constantly, in hopes of becoming part of this exciting new music scene. "For years every morning he'd wake up and be in the mirror rhyming to himself, to hear himself and see how he's pronouncing words and checking his flow," his cousin Be-Hi remembered. "Every morning. You know how some people get up and do they calisthenics every morning? That was his thing."[17] Sometimes Shawn and his friends performed on street corners or at parties. He eventually became known throughout his neighborhood as a talented rapper.

Shawn's growing reputation gave him opportunities to work with other up-and-coming hip-hop artists. When he was eighteen, for instance, he began performing with a fellow Marcy resident known as Jaz-O or Big Jaz. When Jaz signed a contract to cut an album for the EMI record label in 1989, he asked Shawn to appear on it. Shawn rapped on the song "Hawaiian Sophie,"

Jay-Z met Christopher Wallace, later known as the Notorious B.I.G., while at the prestigious George Westinghouse Technical High School.

which was played on the radio in New York City and became a minor hit. He also appeared on the song "Show and Prove" by Brooklyn recording artist Big Daddy Kane.

Decides to Focus on Rap

With each successful collaboration, Shawn continued to build a following among the city's hip-hop fans and expand his contacts in the music business. Many people he met were impressed by his willingness to work hard to improve upon his natural abilities. "He was ambitious and he wanted to get better every day," recalled DJ and record producer Clark Kent. "And it's funny how effortlessly it came to him. He's just gifted."[18]

As his music career showed signs of blossoming, Shawn lost interest in both selling drugs and doing schoolwork. He decided to drop out of high school and quit hustling drugs to focus on his dream of becoming a recording artist. Although it was hard to give up the comfortable lifestyle that drug money provided, Shawn was tired of worrying about getting killed or thrown in prison. He got a legitimate job as a cook at a fast-food restaurant and started saving money to record his own album.

After working for several years, Shawn finally earned enough to pay for sessions in a recording studio. In 1995 he recorded his first original song, "In My Lifetime," and had it turned into a single. The lyrics told a gritty, realistic story about growing up in the projects and working as a drug dealer. Shawn—now known as Jay-Z—worked hard to promote the song. He sold copies from the trunk of his car in the streets of Brooklyn. He also took copies into radio stations and nightclubs and convinced DJs to play it.

In the meantime, Jay-Z continued recording songs with the hope of putting together an entire album. His work attracted the attention of a couple of record labels that offered to help him produce and promote the album. Jay-Z knew that signing a contract with a label would allow him to rent a top recording studio and give his album widespread distribution. But he also knew that powerful record companies sometimes took advantage of promising young artists. They often limited new artists' creative control by insisting that they work with established record producers. They also typically took a large chunk of the profits from album sales in exchange for arranging concert tours, making videos, and other promotional activities. Jay-Z understood the pitfalls of the music business from watching friends like Jaz-O release successful albums without earning much money. He decided to take a risk and try a different approach.

Forms His Own Record Label

Rather than sign a contract with a big record label, Jay-Z decided to form his own label. Along with two partners, Damon Dash and Kareem "Biggs" Burke, he launched Roc-A-Fella Records in early 1996. It was one of a growing number of independent record labels that were formed around that time.

Dash had gained experience in the music industry as a promoter, so he handled the day-to-day business operations at Roc-A-Fella. Burke had a talent for tracking the latest news on the street, so he worked to keep the label at the forefront of hip-hop trends and styles. The first step in building Roc-A-Fella into a successful business, however, involved releasing Jay-Z's debut album. To guarantee that the record would get into stores, the partners ultimately signed a distribution deal with Priority Records. Priority produced the album and handled distribution, but Jay-Z retained full creative control.

Releases His First Album

The result of his hard work, *Reasonable Doubt,* was released in June 1996. It featured fifteen tracks that provided a highly personal account of his experiences as a drug dealer. Jay-Z rapped about the financial rewards of that life as well as the dangers. His realism and clever wordplay made the album an immediate hit. It earned gold record status within three months by selling more than five hundred thousand copies, and it climbed as high as number 23 on the weekly pop chart published by *Billboard* magazine. The album eventually went on to earn platinum status with lifetime sales of more than one million copies.

Damon Dash, right, launched Roc-A-Fella Records with Jay-Z, left, and Kareem Burke in 1996.

In addition to the solid sales figures, *Reasonable Doubt* received high praise from music critics. AllMusic.com reviewer Steve Huey called it "an instant classic of a debut, detailing his experiences

Damon Dash, left, Jay-Z, center, and Kareem Burke pose with gold records, including one for Jay-Z's album Reasonable Doubt.

on the streets with disarming honesty, and writing some of the most acrobatic rhymes heard in quite some time."[19]

The first single from the album to appear on the *Billboard* charts was "Ain't No Nigga (Like the One I Got)," which featured the female rapper Foxy Brown. Although Jay-Z's lyrics were playful and humorous, and the song had a danceable beat, many people objected to the obscene language in the title. Some radio stations refused to play the song, while others edited the word out or replaced it with "brother" or "player." The controversy actually increased the song's popularity, and it remained at the top of the dance charts for five weeks. Other singles that received a lot of airplay included "Dead Presidents" and "Can't Knock the Hustle," which featured guest vocals by Mary J. Blige.

While Jay-Z appreciated the good reviews and sales figures for his first album, he was most gratified by the way his work seemed to connect with hip-hop fans. His songs held great meaning for some people, especially those who shared his experience of growing up in a tough urban neighborhood. "There were cats coming up to me like, 'You must have been looking in my window or following my life,'" he related. "It was emotional. Like big, rough hoodlum, hard rock, three-time jail bidders with scars and gold teeth just breaking down. It was something to look at, like I must be going somewhere people been wanting someone to go for a while."[20]

Chapter 2

Hitting It Big in Rap Music

With the successful release of his first album, *Reasonable Doubt*, Jay-Z established himself as a promising new rap artist. He was determined to build upon this success and become a huge star. During the late 1990s—a time when the world of hip-hop music lost two of its most influential figures to violence—Jay-Z released a series of albums that sold millions of copies and earned multiple Grammy nominations. He also expanded his business interests to include clothing and films. Shortly before the decade ended, however, Jay-Z became entangled in a violent incident that placed his future in jeopardy.

Works on a Follow-up Album

Jay-Z's successful debut album turned Roc-A-Fella Records into a player in the rap music industry. The hit record gave the fledgling independent label instant credibility and visibility. Before long, both powerful record companies and up-and-coming rap artists were clamoring to work with Roc-A-Fella. Jay-Z and his partners took advantage of the opportunity to grow their business. In early 1997 they signed a joint venture agreement with Def Jam, the record company that had brought rap music to a large audience by promoting such early stars as Run DMC and LL Cool J.

The deal put Def Jam in charge of promotion but ensured that Roc-A-Fella maintained creative control. The two companies also

A feud between East Coast and West Coast rappers turned fatal when both Tupac Shakur, left, and the Notorious B.I.G., right, were killed within a few months of each other.

agreed to share ownership rights to all original or master recordings, meaning that they would each receive fifty percent of the profits from future uses of copyrighted songs. After finalizing the deal, Roc-A-Fella worked to find and promote new talent, such as Brooklyn rapper Memphis Bleek. The label also planned a three-volume series of albums by its premier artist, Jay-Z.

While Jay-Z was working on his second album, violence rocked the world of rap music. A high-profile feud between East Coast and West Coast rappers had spiraled to the point that two rap giants—Tupac Shakur and the Notorious B.I.G. (also known as Biggie Smalls)—were shot and killed within a few months of each other. Jay-Z went to high school with the Notorious B.I.G. and worked with him on the song "Brooklyn's Finest," which had appeared on *Reasonable Doubt*. The death of his friend affected Jay-Z deeply. He wanted to honor Biggie's legacy by helping to heal the divisions in the rap world. But he also hoped to claim Biggie's title as the greatest star on the East Coast scene.

Violence in the Rap World

The reputation of rap music suffered greatly in the mid-1990s following several heavily publicized incidents of violence involving rappers from the East and West Coasts of the United States. The West Coast rappers, centered in Los Angeles and under contract with Death Row Records, included Tupac Shakur, Snoop Dogg, and Dr. Dre. The East Coast rappers, centered in New York City and under contract with Bad Boy Records, were led by the Notorious B.I.G. and Sean "Puffy" Combs. Many of these artists released songs that featured violent lyrics and threats or insults aimed at their rivals across the country.

The most high-profile feud involved Tupac Shakur and the Notorious B.I.G. In 1994 Tupac was shot during a trip to New York and claimed that Bad Boy Records was responsible. The Notorious B.I.G. denied the charge and made fun of Tupac in his song "Who Shot Ya?" The following year, Tupac responded with "Hit 'Em Up," in which he insulted the Notorious B.I.G.'s wife, singer Faith Evans.

The feud culminated in the murder of Tupac in Las Vegas in September 1996, followed by the murder of the Notorious B.I.G. six months later in Los Angeles. Both cases went unsolved. The deaths of the two prominent artists hit the rap world hard. Many people demanded an end to the violence and called on rappers to settle their disputes with words rather than guns.

To achieve these goals, Jay-Z worked with one of the best record producers in the business, Sean Combs (also known as Puff Daddy, Puffy, P Diddy, and Diddy). During their recording sessions, Jay-Z's ability to compose entire songs within minutes and commit them to memory amazed Combs. "He writes in his head. You'll hear grunts and 'Woo!'—like he's impressed with what he's writing," the producer recalled. "Of course you're watching; you feel a little left out, like, 'Let me hear what you're saying!' But he keeps writing, then he goes into a [recording] booth."[21]

Releases *In My Lifetime: Volume 1*

Jay-Z released the result of his and Combs' collaboration, *In My Lifetime: Volume 1,* in September 1997. As the title suggests, the album featured a number of songs about Jay-Z's youth and early rap career. The album contained some hardcore rap songs, but most of the tracks had a more mainstream, pop-oriented sound than those on his first album. Some listeners complained that the lighter tone meant that Jay-Z was selling out his existing fans to reach a wider audience. They claimed

Jay-Z worked with record producer Sean "P. Diddy" Combs on the popular album In My Lifetime: Volume 1.

that he had lost some of his street credibility in his attempt to create a crossover hit.

Some reviewers, however, praised Jay-Z for exploring more mature themes in *Volume 1*. They felt that he struck a good balance between respecting his ghetto roots and moving on to address other concerns. Several songs on the album focused on the challenges Jay-Z faced in his new life as a successful recording artist and owner of a record label. In the track "Lucky Me," for instance, he revealed some of the negative aspects of life as a famous rapper. Even though he was wealthy and successful, he noted that he did not feel much safer than he had when he had been a drug dealer. The violence swirling around the world of rap at the time had even convinced him to wear a bulletproof vest while on stage or at parties.

Jay-Z used another song on the album to smooth over the rivalries that had led to violent conflict in the rap world. He collaborated with West Coast rapper Too $hort on the song "Real Niggaz," which paid respects to both Tupac Shakur and the Notorious B.I.G. The lyrics declared that the East-West feud had gone too far when it resulted in the tragic deaths of such talented artists. Elsewhere on the album, Jay-Z asserted his claim to Biggie's throne in the track "The City Is Mine." Featuring a sample from the rock song "You Belong to the City" by Glenn Frey, the song declared that Jay-Z had paid his dues and was ready to take control.

Hip-hop fans cast their votes by snapping up more than one million copies of *Volume 1,* lifting it to the number three position on the pop charts. Despite its popularity, however, Jay-Z later admitted that he was not altogether satisfied with the album. Of all his works, he said *Volume 1* was the one he wished he could do over again. "It was this close to being a classic," he noted, "but I put, like, a few songs on there that ruined it."[22]

Hits It Big with *Volume 2: Hard Knock Life*

Jay-Z felt no such regrets about his next album, *Volume 2: Hard Knock Life*. It sold more than four million copies, won a Grammy Award for Best Rap Album, and launched him to a new level

Jay-Z's Grammy Award winning third album was supported by the Hard Knock Life tour. The tour included rappers Redman (left front), DMX (in camoflauge), and Methodman, center.

of stardom. Anticipation for the album started building in the spring of 1998, when the first single was released. In "Hard Knock Life (Ghetto Anthem)," Jay-Z used samples from the children's chorus of the hit Broadway musical *Annie*. He had actually seen the play as a boy, and he remembered feeling inspired by the strength and courage of the characters—a group of poor children living in an orphanage. "These kids sang about the hard knock life, things everyone in the ghetto feels coming up," he explained. "That's the ghetto anthem."[23] Jay-Z decided to rap over the original version of the song with lyrics about his own tough childhood.

"Hard Knock Life (Ghetto Anthem)" turned out to be a huge hit for Jay-Z. It dominated radio station playlists all summer long and created a surge of interest in the upcoming album. When *Volume 2* was finally released in September 1998, it debuted at number one on the *Billboard* album charts and remained in the top spot for five weeks. It produced a number of other hit singles as well, including "Can I Get a …," "Jigga What," and "Money Ain't a Thing."

Jay-Z collaborated with a number of well-known artists on *Volume 2*. He used beats from hot producers like Timbaland, Kid Capri, and Just Blaze, and he featured vocals from guest rappers like Foxy Brown, Jermaine Dupri, DMX, Ja Rule, and Memphis Bleek. In fact, Jay-Z only rapped by himself on two of the album's fourteen tracks. Some critics charged that he relied too heavily on the contributions of other artists, which diluted the overall impact of the album. "At his best, he shows no fear," wrote a reviewer for AllMusic.com. "Witness how the title track shamelessly works a Broadway showstopper from *Annie* into a raging ghetto cry, yet keeps it smooth enough for radio. It's a stunning single, but unfortunately, it promises more than the rest of the album can deliver."[24] Despite such criticism, however, *Volume 2* turned Jay-Z into a dominant force in the world of hip-hop. *Rolling Stone* magazine recognized his position by naming him the Best Hip-Hop Artist of the Year for 1998.

Jay-Z launched a major concert tour in support of his third album. The Hard Knock Life tour sold out stadium-sized venues in all fifty-two cities it visited. Some cities were reluctant to host hip-hop concerts because they worried that the recent violence in the rap world would spill over to these events. But Jay-Z's tour remained peaceful throughout its run, which helped open more concert venues to hardcore rap performers. In 2000 Roc-A-Fella released a documentary film about the Hard Knock Life tour called *Backstage*. In addition to concert footage, it gave viewers a behind-the-scenes look at Jay-Z and the other performers in the recording studio and on the road.

Faces Criticism for Themes and Lyrics

As Jay-Z rocketed to the top of the charts, he also became a target of criticism from conservative groups. These critics expressed concerns about some of the themes in Jay-Z's work and in rap

Defending his work, Jay-Z claimed rap artists help give people insight into the problems facing African Americans.

music in general. They worried that young people who listened to *Volume 2: Hard Knock Life* might be influenced by Jay-Z's views about drugs, sex, and violence. The Christian group Focus on the Family referred to the album as "garbage" and warned parents not to let their children listen to it.

Jay-Z defended his work against such criticism. He argued that rappers had every right to write songs about drugs and violence because these things were common in their life experience. "We came up from the projects, urban neighborhoods," he explained. "It's not a coincidence that 80 percent of rappers have—if they didn't do it themselves—they've definitely seen somebody deal [drugs]. They was around it. They was in the car when it happened, they was in the hall when it happened. And then people condemn us for the music we make. All we doing is turning a light on in a dark place."[25]

Jay-Z claimed that he and other rap artists gave hip-hop fans greater insight into—and respect for—the problems facing poor African Americans living in the nation's largest cities. "I think the music speaks more directly to youth culture than any other music," he declared. "People that never lived [in the ghetto], they can just pick up a CD and experience the whole thing without having to get shot at."[26] Jay-Z also dismissed the idea that listening to rap music would encourage fans to go out and deal drugs or commit violent crimes. "It's entertainment, and I trust the listener is smart enough to know that," he stated. "I'm just a human being. I do wrong things too and I hope you don't follow me."[27]

Releases *Volume 3: The Life and Times of S. Carter*

In midst of this controversy in 1999, Jay-Z released the first single from his next album, *Volume 3: The Life and Times of S. Carter*. The song, "Big Pimpin'," was a pop-oriented dance tune that featured several guest rappers. It became yet another in Jay-Z's string of hit records. But it also added fuel to fires of criticism surrounding the themes in his music. The lyrics to the

A Short History of Hip-Hop

Hip-hop music began with DJs at nightclubs and house parties. They played different records on two or more turntables at the same time and mixed the sounds together to create a new form of music. Before long, MCs added words to the beat. The vocal element of hip-hop music became known as rap.

The first rap recording hit the Top 40 on the *Billboard* charts in 1979. It was "Rapper's Delight" by the New Jersey-based Sugarhill Gang. By the mid-1980s, hip-hop music could be heard on radio stations across the country. The music industry recognized hip-hop's legitimacy in 1989, when *Billboard* magazine established a new category for rap records and the Recording Industry of America presented the first-ever Grammy Award for Best Rap Performance to DJ Jazzy Jeff and the Fresh Prince (Will Smith) for their song "Parents Just Don't Understand."

Members of the Sugarhill Gang had the first rap recording to hit the Top 40 on the Billboard *charts in 1979.*

Although some critics insisted that rap music was a fad that would soon pass, its popularity grew throughout the 1990s and 2000s. Hip-hop culture gradually evolved to influence American fashion, language, and lifestyle. The best-known hip-hop artists became idols with the power to shape the thinking of a generation of young fans.

song praised the lifestyle of pimps and made it sound cool to treat women disrespectfully.

When Jay-Z released *Volume 3* in late 1999, it received mixed reviews. Some critics felt that it was too slow and claimed that the lyrics were not as clever as those on *Volume 2*. But many others found the album to be a solid addition to Jay-Z's body of work. "This is his strongest album to date," declared a reviewer for *Rolling Stone,* "with music that's filled with catchy hooks, rump-shaking beats, and lyrics fueled by Jay's hustler's vigilance."[28] Jay-Z's growing fan base agreed with this assessment. They bought enough copies to lift *Volume 3* to the top of the *Billboard* charts.

With four successful albums to his name, Jay-Z earned a spot among the most popular and influential stars in rap music. Some people wondered whether being rich and famous would hurt his credibility with hip-hop fans. Jay-Z acknowledged that his life had changed, but he insisted that he remained the same person he had been when he lived in the Marcy Projects. "With five million records out there, there are all kinds of things that you have to deal with," he noted. "People think that things change with you and start treating you differently. Street people start thinking that maybe you've gone soft. But I'm the same dude."[29]

Launches Rocawear Clothing Line

As Jay-Z's fame and popularity grew, he and his business partners took advantage of the opportunity to expand Roc-A-Fella Records into new areas. All three partners wanted Roc-A-Fella to be more than just a record label. They hoped to grow the business beyond music to tap into the surging popularity of hip-hop culture.

Many fans of rap music wanted to copy the image and lifestyle presented by their favorite stars, and they were willing to pay good money to do so. When the group Run DMC appeared in music videos wearing Adidas sneakers, for example, many people rushed out to buy them. But while Adidas benefitted from the group's popularity, Run DMC did not earn money from the sale of the shoes. Jay-Z and his partners decided to develop their own clothing line so that they could keep the profits from this kind of cross-marketing opportunity.

Roc-A-Fella launched a line of urban clothing called Rocawear. Supported by the rappers on the label, the clothing line became a favorite among fans and profits soared.

In 1999 the Roc-A-Fella partners launched a line of urban fashions called Rocawear. Since they did not have any experience producing clothing, they initially considered making a deal with an established apparel manufacturer. In the end, though, they decided that they wanted more control—and more of the profits—than these companies were willing to offer. "In the beginning, we really wanted a deal with a clothing line because I would wear Iceberg [apparel] to shows and when we would get to shows, we'd see the entire audience in Iceberg. We went to Iceberg and wanted to make a deal with them, but at that point, we hadn't sold a significant amount of records," Jay-Z recalled. "When they didn't want to do the deal, we said, 'OK, we'll do it ourselves.'"[30]

Jay-Z and other well-known Roc-A-Fella artists wore Rocawear clothing in their concert appearances, interviews, photo sessions, and music videos. The artists increased the visibility and appeal of the Rocawear brand. Before long, hip-hop fans across the country were rushing out to buy the items they saw their favorite rappers wearing. Sales of Rocawear clothing took off, growing from $8 million in 1999 to $150 million in 2000.

Jay-Z and his partners used a similar approach to expand Roc-A-Fella's business interests to include films. Many of the record label's artists appeared in the 1998 movie, produced by Roc-A-Fella, *Streets Is Watching*, which was shot at Marcy Projects in Brooklyn. Loosely based on Jay-Z's experiences, the film provided viewers with a gritty, realistic picture of life on the streets. In some ways it resembled a series of music videos, with performances by Jay-Z and other rappers. Using Jay-Z's popularity to draw audiences to the film, *Streets Is Watching* brought increased exposure to other Roc-A-Fella artists and their music.

Charged with Stabbing a Rival Rapper

By the end of 1999 Jay-Z's successful albums, concert tours, and business ventures had pushed him to the forefront of hip-hop culture. But in December of that year, he was involved in a violent incident that threatened everything he had worked so hard to achieve. The incident occurred at a glitzy nightclub called the Kit Kat Klub on Times Square in New York City. Jay-Z went there to help fellow rapper Q-Tip, a member of the group A Tribe Called Quest, celebrate the release of his solo album *Amplified*.

Many of the biggest names in rap music attended the star-studded event. One of the guests at the party was Lance "Un"

Rivera of Undeas Entertainment. Several months earlier, Rivera had produced a song for Jay-Z. Jay-Z was convinced that Rivera had sold bootleg copies of the record before it became available in stores. Although Rivera denied the charge, hard feelings still existed between the two men.

Jay-Z, right, being arrested in 1999 in connection with a nightclub fight where music producer Lance Rivera was stabbed.

At one point in the evening, a fight broke out in the Kit Kat Klub. During the scuffle, Rivera was stabbed in the stomach and hit over the head with a champagne bottle. He claimed that Jay-Z was responsible for the attack. Jay-Z was arrested and charged with assault. Rivera also filed a civil lawsuit that, if successful, would force Jay-Z to pay monetary damages for Rivera's injuries and suffering.

The charges leveled at Jay-Z were very serious. If he was convicted, he faced up to fifteen years in prison. But Jay-Z consistently denied attacking Rivera. He said that he could produce eyewitnesses and a security video that proved he was nowhere near his rival when the fight broke out. The legal wrangling between the two sides dragged on for months, with every new development splashed across the pages of tabloid magazines.

Faces the Music

As the legal drama surrounding the stabbing incident unfolded, Rivera became less confident about the identity of his attacker. He eventually dropped his civil lawsuit against Jay-Z, but the authorities still seemed determined to take the criminal case to trial. Jay-Z was convinced that the officials in charge of prosecuting the case enjoyed the attention that it brought them. "The DA [district attorney] has a publicist. Did you know that? That's unreal to me," he declared. "That's not justice, that's drama."[31]

By the end of 2001 Jay-Z decided that he was tired of fighting and just wanted the case to be over. He also expressed doubt that he would receive a fair trial because of his race, and he was not willing to take the risk of being convicted and sent to prison. "Where I grew up, I saw a lot of people get wronged," he claimed. "No matter how much you believe in the truth, that's always in the back of your mind."[32] Given all these considerations, Jay-Z agreed to plead guilty to a lesser charge and accepted a punishment of three years' probation.

Jay-Z later claimed that the whole experience affected his outlook on life. He realized that he could have lost everything he had worked so hard to achieve. It made him appreciate his success in a deeper way, and it made him determined to be more careful in the future. "That was the turning point for me," he acknowledged. "It was like, 'OK, this can all go away fast. You work hard for years, and it can all go away in a night. Slow down, big boy. Think.'"[33]

Chapter 3

Retiring as a Rap Artist

As the hit songs continued to pile up for Jay-Z, he also gained a greater awareness of the downside of fame. Legal troubles and heated feuds with other rappers dogged him throughout the early 2000s. Meanwhile, Jay-Z expanded his business interests into new areas, such as clothing, restaurants, and beverages. Over time, he decided to quit recording and performing as a rap artist and focus on new challenges. He retired in 2003 with a great deal of fanfare, culminating his recording career with an acclaimed final album and a hugely successful farewell concert in Madison Square Garden.

Focuses on His Work

During the time that the Rivera assault case wound its way through the courts, Jay-Z kept his head down, stayed out of trouble, and focused on his work. In October 2000 he released an album called *Dynasty—Roc La Familia*. The album mainly served as a showcase for lesser-known artists on the Roc-A-Fella label, although it featured a few new songs by Jay-Z.

The biggest hit single from *Dynasty* was the Jay-Z song "I Just Wanna Love U (Give It 2 Me)." Built around a sample from "Give It to Me Baby," a classic funk song by Rick James, it created a sensation on dance floors across the country. The song's popularity helped lift the album to the top spot on the

Throughout his assault case, Jay-Z remained focused on his music.

Billboard charts, making Jay-Z the first artist in twenty-five years to post two number-one albums within a year, because *Volume 3: The Life and Times of S. Carter* was still at number one at the beginning of 2000. On the more personal side, *Dynasty* also featured the song "Where Have You Been?" In this duet, Jay-Z and fellow rapper Beanie Sigel shared their feelings about growing up without fathers.

Releases *The Blueprint*

Although *Dynasty* sold more than two million copies, some of Jay-Z's fans were disappointed by how little he was featured on the album. They were hungry for a major new album by their favorite rapper. Jay-Z delivered in September 2001 with *The Blueprint.* To the delight of his fans, Jay-Z rapped alone on every song but one ("Renegade," which featured guest vocals from Eminem). He also increased the complexity of his rhymes and the seriousness of his subject matter, while toning down the violent and sexist content of his lyrics.

As Jay-Z grew as an artist, he featured more complex, serious, and personal lyrics in his songs.

The Blueprint became a huge hit with fans and critics alike. It debuted at number one on the *Billboard* charts, selling 450,000 copies in the first week. Critics called it an instant classic and the best album of Jay-Z's career. In a review for *All Music Guide,* for instance, Jason Birchmeier described *The Blueprint*'s thirteen tracks as "stunning, to the point where the album almost seems flawless.... A fully realized masterpiece."34

Many critics were struck by the album's deeply personal songs. Jay-Z discussed such meaningful topics as his feelings about his mother, his legal problems, and his struggles to establish a strong romantic relationship. Other critics praised Jay-Z for moving hip-hop toward a more sophisticated sound. Many songs on the album featured samples from vintage soul and rhythm-and-blues (R&B) records.

A few reviewers, however, criticized Jay-Z for presenting himself on *The Blueprint* as the god of the rap world. He introduced himself as "J-Hova" or "H.O.V.A.," taken from Jehovah—the proper name of God from the Old Testament of the Bible. In a review for *Rolling Stone,* Neil Strauss claimed that Jay-Z may have felt compelled to build himself up after all the negative publicity that surrounded the assault case. "There's something about being persecuted, or at least believing oneself to be persecuted, that makes people embrace and reaffirm their own identity—witness Jay-Z's sixth album, *The Blueprint,*" he wrote. "Personal and legal problems have provoked Jay-Z to write what may be his most personal, straightforward album but also his most self-aggrandizing work."35

Feuds with Nas

Besides his legal troubles, Jay-Z had other reasons to feel a need to defend himself on *The Blueprint.* His many successes had drawn the attention of rival rappers, and he had become a major target for insults and threats in the ongoing battle of words in the rap world. Although the bitter feud between East Coast and West Coast rappers had ended following the violent deaths of Tupac Shakur and the Notorious B.I.G., new rivalries developed between various artists vying for supremacy on the East Coast scene.

The rivalry between Nas and Jay-Z led to verbal attacks and insults back and forth in different interviews and songs.

A number of fellow New York rappers attacked Jay-Z in their work, including Jadakiss, DMX, Nas, and Prodigy of Mobb Deep.

The heated exchanges between Jay-Z and Nas turned their two-year-long battle into one of the most celebrated rap feuds in history. The two rappers traded jabs in interviews, concert appearances, and on the radio. Jay-Z made his feelings about Nas clear in "Takeover," the opening track on *The Blueprint*. The song had a military beat and featured a sample from The Doors song "Five to One." The lyrics questioned Nas's street credibility and suggested that he had invented his ghetto background. Jay-Z also attacked Nas's talent as a rapper and claimed that his latest releases belonged in the trash. Finally, Jay-Z asserted his own superiority and presented himself as the dominant figure on the New York rap scene.

Jay-Z insisted that his attacks on Nas and other rivals were simply part of the battle-rap tradition. He claimed that he ignored their insults as long as possible but finally had to fight back in order to gain their respect. "Everybody wants to be respected," he explained. "Even if we're not friends, we gotta respect each other. And I felt I was bein' disrespected by them, so I had to show them. And I really waited it out because I didn't want people to think I was a bully. Because I have the ear of a lot more people than them. You have to be very careful with that power.... I'm sure they respect me right now."[36]

Shortly after the release of *The Blueprint*, Nas answered "Takeover" in his song "Ether." He focused his criticism on the sexist lyrics and attitudes he saw in Jay-Z's work. He insinuated that these themes showed that Jay-Z felt some deep-seated anger or fear toward women, perhaps because he had been abused as a child or had secret homosexual tendencies. Jay-Z responded to "Ether" with "Super Ugly," a freestyle rap that first aired on a New York radio station and later appeared on the live album *Jay-Z Unplugged*. In this song, Jay-Z viciously attacked Nas by claiming that he had an affair with the mother of Nas's child.

Although the two rappers continued to exchange glancing verbal blows afterward, "Super Ugly" marked the end of their all-out feud. Many people felt that Jay-Z had gone too far in the song. Even his own mother called to tell him that she found it mean-spirited. Nas never responded to the song formally, although he did make critical comments about it in interviews. The conflict eventually faded to the point that the two rappers decided to make peace. Both Jay-Z and Nas agreed to perform at a 2005 concert sponsored by a New York radio station. The two rappers made a joint appearance on stage and shook hands to officially bring their feud to a close.

Releases *The Blueprint 2*

Jay-Z continued to discuss some of the negative aspects of fame in his next album, *The Blueprint 2: The Gift and the Curse*. By November 2002, when the album was released, he had settled the assault case and cooled his battle of words with Nas.

But Jay-Z still faced the challenge of maintaining his identity—which had been forged by poverty and pain—while also enjoying the rewards of his success. This struggle became the overall theme of *The Blueprint 2*. "The gift-versus-curse concept helps hold things together," noted one reviewer, "as Jay wows you with his jet-setting lifestyle one minute, then contemplates the darker side of fame and his ghetto upbringing the next."[37]

By all appearances, Jay-Z had a great deal to say on the subject. *The Blueprint 2* was a double album, containing twenty-five tracks and employing the talents of a small army of producers and guest vocalists. It spawned several hit singles, including "'03 Bonnie and Clyde" (a duet with Beyoncé) and "Guns and Roses" (a duet with Lenny Kravitz), and sold an impressive four million copies.

Despite its strong sales, *The Blueprint 2* was not nearly as popular with critics as its predecessor. Many reviewers complained that the double album was too long and unfocused. They claimed that it only contained enough quality material for a single album. Jay-Z responded to this criticism five months later by releasing *The Blueprint 2.1*. This album contained half of the tracks from *The Blueprint 2,* along with two new, previously unreleased songs.

Decides to Retire

With the release of *The Blueprint 2.1* in 2003, Jay-Z's output spanned nine albums that collectively sold more than thirty million copies. Although he seemed to have a magic touch for connecting with hip-hop fans, he recognized that this might not be the case as he grew older. "I think, unfortunately, rap music is made to destroy itself," he stated. "You have to be fresh and sell to an audience that's 16 to 25. They demand that you 'keep it hood,' 'keep it real.'"[38]

Jay-Z's success as a recording artist, meanwhile, had provided him with numerous opportunities to expand his business interests. His Rocawear clothing brand had posted an incredible $300 million in sales in 2003 alone. The company planned to introduce new lines of apparel for women and children. In addition, Jay-Z became one of the main backers of a chain of sports

Jay-Z "retired" from rapping and expanded his business interests, including investing in the 40/40 Club, an upscale sports bar.

bars called the 40/40 Club that opened in New York and Atlantic City in 2003. Roc-A-Fella also branched out into beverages by becoming a distributor for Armandale vodka.

Jay-Z also found himself in demand among companies that wanted him to endorse their products. He accepted an offer from Reebok to help design and promote his own signature line of shoes, the S. Carter collection. Jay-Z thus became the first celebrity from outside the world of sports to have his own athletic shoe. The first model introduced by Reebok in 2003 sold out within a week, making it the fastest-selling shoe in the company's history.

Between managing his business empire and promoting new artists on the Roc-A-Fella record label, Jay-Z found that he did

Reaching Out to His Father

As he put plans in place to retire as a recording artist, Jay-Z also achieved some closure in his personal life. In 2003—after being out of contact for more than twenty years—Jay-Z reconciled with his father, Adnes Reeves.

His mother, Gloria Carter, encouraged Jay-Z to reach out because she knew that her former husband was in poor health. The two men met several times before Reeves died of liver disease. Jay-Z acknowledged that the meetings were painful at first, but he appreciated the opportunity to tell his father how he felt about being abandoned. "I was really hard on the guy all these years," he noted. "My feelings were hurt." His father apologized for his actions, and Jay-Z was able to put the negative feelings behind him.

Source: Quoted in Emma Forrest, "Jay-Z: Hip-Hop's Hottest Guy Talks about It All," *Teen People*, June 16, 2002, p. 54.

not have much time to devote to making new albums. He eventually decided to retire as a recording artist to concentrate on new challenges. "I've had it with the rap game. Time to focus on other things. That's why I'm retiring," he explained. "I've talked about wanting to have enough to get out since my first album. I was always more interested in the business side."[39]

Goes Out with a Bang

Determined to go out on top, Jay-Z began working on his farewell album, which he called *The Black Album*. He decided to return to his roots and create a prequel to his first album, *Reasonable Doubt*. *The Black Album* was released in November 2003. The opening track, called "December 4th," after his birthday, featured spoken-word interludes from his mother. Later tracks continued to tell the story of his life.

Rapping with The Beatles

Mixing different kinds of music together is an important element of hip-hop. In recognition of this, Jay-Z and other rap artists often make stripped-down versions of their songs available for other artists to sample in their work. For example, Jay-Z released the vocal tracks from his *The Black Album*—without the accompanying music—in hopes that other rappers would use them in mashups and mixes.

A British DJ known as Danger Mouse combined the raps from Jay-Z's *The Black Album* with samples from the classic Beatles release known as *The White Album*. The result became known as *The Grey Album*. As it turned out, though, Danger Mouse did not have permission from EMI—the label that held the legal rights to the Beatles music—to use songs from *The White Album*. EMI filed a legal action to force the DJ and record sellers to stop distributing *The Grey Album*. The swirl of controversy surrounding the album only increased its popularity, however, and it became a huge underground hit.

Inspired by *The Grey Album*, other enterprising music lovers created *The Grey Video*. This popular Internet movie combined footage from various Jay-Z music videos with footage from The Beatles' film *A Hard Day's Night*. At least one former Beatle seemed to appreciate the connection with Jay-Z. Paul McCartney agreed to appear on stage with the rap star at the Grammy Awards. They performed an innovative combination of the Beatles song "Yesterday" with the song "Numb/Encore" by Jay-Z and Linkin Park.

Jay-Z performing with Sir Paul McCartney in 2006.

Critics described *The Black Album* as an honest and introspective work that stood as a fitting conclusion for Jay-Z's recording career. "Given one last chance to make an impact, Jay-Z has come up with one of the better albums of his career,"[40] noted a reviewer for *Rolling Stone*. *The Black Album* sold three million copies and spawned a number of hit singles, including "What More Can I Say," "Change Clothes," and "99 Problems," which earned Jay-Z a Grammy Award for Best Rap Solo Performance.

The Black Album also featured the dance tune "Dirt Off Your Shoulder," which entered mainstream popular culture in a way that few rap songs ever had before. Jay-Z's lyrics suggested that the best way for people to deal with criticism was to brush it off, like they would brush a speck of dirt from their shoulder. This idea became the basis for a brushing gesture that could be used in response to critics. In 2008 Senator Barack Obama even used the gesture during his successful presidential campaign to show how he intended to deal with criticism from his political rivals.

Gives a Memorable Farewell Concert

Jay-Z followed up on the success of *The Black Album* by announcing that he would culminate his career with a triumphant farewell concert, with all of the proceeds donated to charity. The Fade to Black concert was scheduled for November 25, 2003, at Madison Square Garden in New York City. This premier concert venue had not hosted a show by a hip-hop artist in fifteen years due to concerns about the potential for violence. But when Jay-Z convinced the Garden to make an exception for his final concert, the 20,000 seats sold out in less than five minutes.

The Fade to Black concert was a star-studded event, from the famous faces in the audience to the wealth of talented performers on stage. The show featured guest appearances by many of Jay-Z's friends and collaborators, including Mary J. Blige, Beyoncé, Missy Elliott, Foxy Brown, R. Kelly, Ghostface Killah, Pharrell Williams, and Beanie Sigel. Jay-Z even invited

During the Fade to Black concert at Madison Square Garden in 2003, Jay-Z invited Afeni Shakur (Tupac Shakur's mother), left, and Voletta Wallace (Notorious B.I.G.'s mother), right, on stage with him.

the mothers of the late rappers Tupac Shakur and the Notorious B.I.G., Voletta Wallace and Afeni Shakur, to join him on stage. He delighted the crowd by playing songs from throughout his career, changing costume five times, and using lots of pyrotechnics.

The spectacular show formed the basis of the 2004 documentary film *Fade to Black*, which also featured behind-the-scenes footage of the performers. Jay-Z claimed that he did not fully appreciate the impact of the event until he watched the movie. "I couldn't feel it at the time. It took for me to watch the movie to really say like 'Wow, that was huge,'" he said. "The emotional aspect kicked in later when I looked at it.... I was blown away."[41] He felt that the film did a great job of tracing the journey "of a kid from Marcy Projects in Brooklyn making it to the biggest stage in the world."[42]

Chapter 4

Becoming a Business Mogul

When Jay-Z announced his retirement in 2003, some fans worried that he was leaving the music business entirely. They thought that his popularity and influence would fade if he stopped rapping and expressed hope that he would reconsider. As it turned out, their fears about Jay-Z's retirement were unfounded. Jay-Z continued to record and perform with other artists. In addition, he made a dramatic move to become one of the most powerful figures in the recording industry. In 2004 he accepted a position as president of Def Jam Records. During his three-year tenure in this position, Jay-Z gained even more credibility and respect in the music industry and helped open new doors for black executives.

Stays Busy in Retirement

Even after he officially retired as a recording artist, Jay-Z stayed busy. In fact, a 2004 *New York Times* profile described him as "the hardest-working retiree in the music industry."[43] Although Jay-Z did not release any new albums under his own name, he continued recording songs with other artists. For instance, he collaborated with Beyoncé—the former lead singer and songwriter for the all-female rhythm-and-blues (R&B) group Destiny's Child—on the hit song "Crazy in Love." It won two Grammy Awards, for Best R&B Song and Best Rap/Sung

Jay-Z accepts the Golden Note Award from the American Society of Composers, Authors, and Publishers on June 28, 2004.

Collaboration. Their performance also fueled intense speculation in the media about whether the two stars were romantically involved.

Jay-Z received further recognition of his talents as an artist when he earned the Golden Note Award from the American Society of Composers, Authors, and Publishers in 2004. The following year, he won another Grammy Award for Best Rap/Sung Collaboration for "Numb/Encore." This song combined parts of the Jay-Z song "Encore" with parts of the song "Numb" by the hard-rock band Linkin Park. It was one of several mashups of existing songs by the artists that appeared on the album *Collision Course,* which was released in November 2004. The album also included a DVD with footage of Jay-Z and Linkin Park performing some of the songs live on MTV.

Jay-Z also collaborated with R&B star R. Kelly on the album *Unfinished Business* during his so-called retirement. It debuted at the number one position on the *Billboard* charts upon its release in 2004. The two artists also planned a forty-city concert tour in support of the album. "Unfortunately, what looked good on paper didn't work out that way in reality,"[44] according to Jay-Z. As soon as they hit the road, the two stars clashed repeatedly. After a few concerts together, Jay-Z kicked R. Kelly off the tour for unprofessional behavior. "It takes a lot to make Jay mad," a friend noted,

R. Kelly, right, and Jay-Z perform during the Best of Both Worlds Tour in 2004. R. Kelly was later kicked off the tour by Jay-Z for unprofessional behavior.

"so the fact that this got to the boiling point shows how bad it was."[45] Jay-Z filled the remaining concert dates with a string of other co-stars, including Usher and Mary J. Blige. R. Kelly later filed a $75 million lawsuit, arguing that Jay-Z had broken a contract by forcing him to leave the tour. A judge decided that there was not enough evidence to make a ruling and threw out the case.

Looks for a New Challenge

Although Jay-Z enjoyed his post-retirement musical collaborations, he still looked for opportunities to challenge himself in other ways. He was particularly interested in expanding his role as a business executive in the recording industry. "The business of business has always been something I focused on, and rightly so," he explained. "Rap is a young man's game, and I thought about that even when I was young—it has to come to an end. Whatever job you have, be it hustling on the street or working at the mall, you gotta have a plan for when it's over."[46]

Jay-Z had gained valuable experience in the music business by running the Roc-A-Fella label. He hoped that this background—combined with the credibility and influence he had built within the industry as a successful rapper—might help him land a powerful position with one of America's giant record companies. Many people in the music business supported the idea. "Who wouldn't want to hire the most popular guy in hip-hop? His face alone would get the deal done," noted one industry executive. "That wouldn't have happened to a kid coming straight out of the ghetto—he never would have had a shot."[47]

Still, Jay-Z was not willing to accept a position that used only his image, rather than his talents. He wanted a hands-on management position that would allow him to influence the future direction of hip-hop music and make a difference in the black community. "What I want to do is have a position that opens the doors for black executives in the music business," he stated. "I don't think there are enough of us. I want to break that glass ceiling. But it has to be a real position, or I'm not doing it. I want to be the black quarterback."[48]

Becomes President of Def Jam Records

Around the time that Jay-Z retired as an artist, a management shakeup occurred at Universal Music Group (UMG). UMG was a giant company in the music industry, with dozens of respected record labels, a huge roster of top artists from all genres of music, and an extensive catalog of copyrighted songs under its

Shortly after being named president of Def Jam, Jay-Z (center left) joins Antonio "L.A." Reid, chairman of Island Def Jam Music Group (right); hip-hop mogul Russell Simmons (center right); and Tony Austin (left) to announce the formation of a new label with Simmons called The Russell Simmons Music Group.

control. UMG also was the parent company of Def Jam Records, which owned half of Roc-A-Fella Records through a 1997 joint venture agreement.

In 2004 several top executives left UMG and moved to rival Warner Music Group. Some of these executives had been involved with Def Jam since the label's early years, and they maintained close relationships with many Def Jam and Roc-A-Fella artists.

Def Jam Records

By the time Jay-Z became president of the company in 2005, Def Jam Records had been at the forefront of hip-hop music and culture for two decades. Russell Simmons and Rick Rubin had founded the record label in 1984 in a dormitory room at New York University. Def Jam earned its trend-setting reputation by promoting such early hip-hop stars as Run DMC, LL Cool J, the Beastie Boys, and Public Enemy. The company signed a distribution deal with Columbia Records in 1985 and grew rapidly in both size and influence.

Jay-Z's first interaction with Def Jam came in 1997. Shortly after the release of his first album, he and his partners in Roc-A-Fella Records signed a joint venture agreement with the larger label. As part of their deal, the two companies also agreed to share ownership rights to all original or master recordings. As Jay-Z released more albums and became a major star, Def Jam benefited from his success.

In 1999 Universal Music Group bought Def Jam. Thanks to strong record sales by Jay-Z and other artists on the label, such as Ludacris, Ja Rule, and Kanye West, Def Jam posted $1 billion in revenue in 2004. That year, however, a number of top executives left Universal and moved to rival Warner Music Group. Concerned that Jay-Z and other Roc-A-Fella artists might be tempted to change labels, Universal cemented the relationship by making Jay-Z the new president of Def Jam.

Becoming a Business Mogul   **59**

This event led to industry rumors that Jay-Z and other rappers would move to Warner, following the executives who had long supported them.

Antonio "L.A." Reid, who became chairman of UMG's Island Def Jam Music Group after the management shakeup, was determined to prevent this from happening. He recognized that the key to keeping existing Def Jam and Roc-A-Fella artists in the fold was to make Jay-Z happy. "Jay being the biggest, most successful, most influential artist on the roster, it became a priority of mine to develop a relationship,"[49] Reid explained.

When Reid learned that Jay-Z was looking for an executive position, he offered the rapper a prestigious job as president of Def Jam Records. "After 10 years of successfully running Roc-A-Fella, Shawn has proved himself to be an astute businessman, in addition to the brilliant artistic talent that the world sees and hears," Reid said in an official press release announcing Jay-Z's appointment. "I can think of no one more relevant and credible in the hip-hop community to build upon Def Jam's fantastic legacy and move the company into its next groundbreaking era."[50]

To convince Jay-Z to take the job, UMG made him a mind-boggling offer. As part of the deal, Def Jam purchased the half of Roc-A-Fella that it did not already own for a rumored $30 million. The company also offered to pay Jay-Z a salary estimated at $10 million per year. Most importantly, UMG agreed to give Jay-Z full control of his master recordings—along with all of the future profits that came from these copyrighted songs—after ten years. Between the sweet financial arrangements and the opportunity to become the first popular artist to take the reins of a major record label, Jay-Z could not resist. He signed a three-year contract to serve as president of Def Jam, beginning in January 2005.

Reid insisted that his company got a good deal as well. "Def Jam is the number one hip-hop label in the world," he stated. "Having Jay says that the legacy continues. If you're a 16-year-old rapper in Brooklyn or Atlanta or Houston, and you know that Jay-Z carries on the legacy of hip-hop, then Def Jam becomes your preferred destination."[51]

Learns on the Job

Upon moving into his plush executive office in the Universal Building, Jay-Z realized that he faced high expectations in his new job. "It's the biggest hip-hop label of all time," he said of Def Jam. "If that thing falls apart, it's on my head. I was naive enough to believe I can do it."[52] Jay-Z also understood that many people questioned whether he had the necessary skills and qualifications to succeed in such a high-profile position. "Any record executive knows that Jay-Z in the boardroom brings

Jay-Z signed a number of talented and successful musicians to Def Jam, including Ne-Yo and Rihanna.

another level of respect from within the industry," said the vice president of another record label. "But the real key isn't just whether or not Jay-Z is able to find and sign the talent. It's whether he can really do the business part, which means staying within budget and bringing in a certain amount of revenue. That's the test for Jay."[53]

Jay-Z was able to draw upon his experience running Roc-A-Fella in adjusting to the demands of his new job. He also received a great deal of help and support from within Def Jam and UMG. UMG management handled most of the high-level contracts, budgets, and financial arrangements for him. Jay-Z also had a staff of seven division heads within Def Jam to take care of the day-to-day aspects of running the business. This left Jay-Z free to focus on what he knew best: the music side of the business. His main job involved finding new artists and turning them into stars. "His opinion of music and his point of view on marketing is absolutely spot on," declared fellow executive Steve Stoute. "I don't know who wouldn't want to work for him."[54]

Jay-Z's Executive Digs

Once Jay-Z became president of Def Jam Records, he immediately established himself as the coolest executive in the music industry. Jay-Z's sense of style shone throughout his L-shaped office on the twenty-ninth floor of the Universal Building in New York City. Large windows on two sides offered a spectacular view of the Hudson River. On the interior walls he placed a big-screen TV, a street sign from Marcy Avenue in Brooklyn, and framed photographs of himself with famous people ranging from singer Mariah Carey to England's Prince Charles. One of the highlights of Jay-Z's office décor was a scale model of Atlantic Yards, the new stadium in Brooklyn where the NBA's New Jersey Nets were scheduled to move in 2011. To top it off, he made sure that the room was always brimming with fresh flowers.

Within months of settling into his new job, Jay-Z signed a number of talented newcomers to record deals with Def Jam, including Young Jeezy, Ne-Yo, Rihanna, and British rapper Lady Sovereign. He also promoted new albums, videos, and concert tours that turned existing artists like Kanye West and Ludacris into huge stars. Jay-Z developed close relationships with many of these artists, and he found it very rewarding to nurture their careers. "I'm not looking to be anybody's boss. I'm just looking to help the process. If they win, I win,"[55] he explained. "I love the process. It's another way of being creative. Especially with a new artist, when somebody walks in and they don't understand what's going on and they are all wide-eyed. Then the next year, they are signing autographs and they're big, too."[56]

Earns Respect

On a typical day at the office, Jay-Z spent several hours scanning radio playlists and album charts, listening to new songs, and advising his artists about career moves. "If Jay-Z says you have to go back in the studio and write new bars, you've got to write new bars," declared Semtex, the urban promotions manager for Def Jam. "If Jay-Z says your stage show isn't hot, it isn't hot. You can't argue with him; he's sold millions of records."[57]

Over time, Jay-Z used his position as head of Def Jam to shift hip-hop culture toward a more mature, sophisticated style. His fans took note of the fact that one of the most successful rappers of all time quit performing to become a recording executive. This decision made the world of business seem cooler and more interesting to many of them. Some of this change in attitude became clear in the subject matter addressed in rap lyrics and the clothing worn by hip-hop fans. "In 'getting his executive on,' as the kids call it these days," wrote one analyst, Jay-Z "is not only redirecting the hip-hop culture he helped popularize—from hooded sweatshirt thug-chic to button-down shirt sophistication—but injecting the music business with a new sensibility."[58]

With Jay-Z as president, Def Jam solidified its position as the most popular and influential hip-hop label. "It's been great," he stated in late 2006. "The first year we had the No. 2 market share and this year, if everything goes right, we'll have the No. 1."[59] The management of Def Jam's parent company, UMG, expressed great satisfaction with Jay-Z's performance. "Jay's put Def Jam back on the map," said UMG executive Doug Morris. "Everything he touches gets cooler."[60]

Chapter 5

Having It All

Despite the rewards of running Def Jam, Jay-Z felt a strong urge to end his retirement and return to the recording studio. His long-awaited comeback album, *Kingdom Come,* was followed by an ambitious, Grammy-nominated concept album inspired by the movie *American Gangster.* By combining business successes with artistic accomplishments, Jay-Z brought the various threads of his career together to reach a new level of power and influence. He also expressed a growing recognition that he could use his wealth and celebrity to have a positive impact on the world.

Ends His Retirement

During his first year as president of Def Jam in 2005, Jay-Z mostly concentrated on his new role and responsibilities as an executive. He continued to come up with ideas for songs and albums that he might want to record someday, but he did not feel a strong desire to return to the studio.

Jay-Z did perform in concert on a few occasions during this period, though. A memorable example came in October 2005, when he headlined the annual Powerhouse concert for the New York radio station Power 105.1. A number of other top Def Jam artists appeared as well, including Kanye West, Young Jeezy, and Ne-Yo. Since the concert was called "I Declare War," many people assumed that Jay-Z would use the show to launch verbal attacks on his biggest rivals. Instead, he made a strong statement that his new executive position placed him above the fray of rap battles.

During a controversial performance in 2006, Jay-Z presented himself as the president—his fans loved it.

During the show, Jay-Z presented himself as the president of the United States. He sat behind a large desk on a stage set that looked like the Oval Office. Surrounded by actors dressed as Secret Service agents in suits, he declared his intention to make peace in the rap world. The highlight of the show came when his longtime rival Nas joined him onstage to officially bring their years-long feud to an end. The two artists performed a mashup of Jay-Z's song "Dead Presidents" and Nas's song "The World Is Yours."

The thrill that Jay-Z felt from these performances made him realize that he needed more than an occasional collaboration or concert appearance to fulfill his love for creating music.

In 2006, less than three years after he retired, Jay-Z returned to the recording studio. "It was the worst retirement, maybe, in history," he acknowledged. "It wasn't like a defining moment. Something, when you love it, is always tugging at you and itching at you, and I was putting it off and putting it off. I started fumbling around to see if it felt good."[61]

Releases *Kingdom Come*

As the president of Def Jam, Jay-Z had access to an all-star group of producers and collaborators, including Dr. Dre, Kanye West, the Neptunes, Chris Martin of Coldplay, John Legend, Usher, Ne-Yo, and Beyoncé. All of these artists were eager to help him with his long-awaited comeback album. Jay-Z named the album *Kingdom Come,* after an old DC Comics series in which Superman returned to Earth after a self-imposed exile to find destruction and chaos. Fans snapped up copies upon its release in November 2006. *Kingdom Come* debuted at number one on the *Billboard* album chart, selling 680,000 copies in the first week, and went on to top two million in sales.

The album spawned several hit singles, including "Show Me What You Got." Many of the songs on the album featured samples from an interesting variety of music. The title track included samples from Rick James's funky dance tune "Super Freak," for instance, while "Oh My God" had samples from the Allman Brothers' blues-rock classic "Whipping Post." To the dismay of some fans who had enjoyed Jay-Z's take on street life, many of his lyrics focused on the rewards of being a high-powered executive. "It wasn't what people wanted to hear," Jay-Z acknowledged. "But it's what I wanted to do. I was trying to show that hip-hop can talk about different things."[62]

Kingdom Come received mixed reviews from critics. Most reviewers agreed that the album had some strong points, but they generally found that Jay-Z's long-awaited comeback failed to live up to expectations. "*Kingdom Come* was hardly the creative flop it was cracked up to be, but it never had a prayer of living up to everybody's hopes," noted one reviewer. "People don't just expect new records from Jay—they expect epochal events, game-changing statements. Yet Jay's retirement put his myth-building on pause."[63]

Finds Inspiration in a Film

After the release of *Kingdom Come,* Jay-Z did not expect to make another album for a while. He was prepared to turn his full attention back to his job at Def Jam. In mid-2007, however, he was inspired to make a new album that returned to his roots. The inspiration came from an unusual source: a movie called *American Gangster.* The film was based on the story of Frank Lucas, a real-life gangster who built a heroin empire in Harlem during the 1970s. It starred Denzel Washington as Lucas and

Jay-Z was inspired in 2007 by the movie American Gangster.

Russell Crowe as the New York City police detective who was determined to bring him to justice.

Jay-Z was invited to an advance screening of the film. He was struck by the parallels with his own story. "The way Denzel portrayed the character was very laid back, and I saw similar traits in my personality," he explained. "But mostly, I just pulled emotions from the film and not so much his particular story. It was the complexity of the human beings that I was drawn to. For most of the movie, you don't know who is the good guy or bad guy."[64]

Watching *American Gangster* inspired Jay-Z to envision how his life might have turned out if he had remained a drug dealer rather than getting into rap music. Before long, he was actively sketching out a concept album that explored this fantasy. He approached Sean "Diddy" Combs to serve as the producer. As it turned out, Combs had been saving a number of good background beats in case a suitable project came along. "I was like, 'Wow, what are you doing with all this stuff?'" Jay-Z remembered. "And he was like, 'Who is going to rap on this but you?'"[65]

Releases *American Gangster*

The resulting album also was called *American Gangster*, even though none of the songs appeared on the soundtrack of the film. It hit the top of the *Billboard* charts upon its release in November 2007. This gave Jay-Z ten career number-one albums, which tied him with Elvis Presley for the most ever by a solo performer (the Beatles held the overall record with nineteen).

The songs on *American Gangster* followed the rise and fall of an imagined drug lord. "Jay's *Gangster* tale follows a striking, dramatic arc of its own, transporting listeners from a young hustler's ambition ('Pray,' 'No Hook') to a kingpin's arrogance ('Roc Boys,' 'Ignorant S—') to a career criminal's inevitable ruin ('Fallin'),"[66] Simon Vozick-Levinson wrote in *Entertainment Weekly*. Since the album was intended to tell a story, Jay-Z did not make the songs available separately as singles. "It's a concept album, not a collection of singles, and I want it heard the way I intended it," he explained. "A painter doesn't sell a section of a painting. He sells a whole body of work."[67]

American Gangster received glowing reviews from critics, who praised the album's originality and passion. "Having a fictional character to play around with gets Jay out of his post-retirement rut," noted one reviewer. "Frank Lucas fires his imagination [and] helps push the artist outside his own head."[68] Jay-Z appreciated the fact that *American Gangster*—which earned a Grammy nod as Best Rap Album—helped restore his reputation as a top recording artist. "With rap, it's always about the next project, no matter who you are! It's about what's current, what's happening right this second," he noted. "[*Gangster*] set the foundation all over again, and it made everybody say, 'Whoa, hold up for a second.' It quelled those arguments [that Jay-Z had lost his touch], and those arguments were not founded, but that's just how it happens. That's what keeps it fresh for me. I love that challenge."[69]

Leaves Def Jam for New Business Opportunities

Shortly after the release of *American Gangster*, Jay-Z's love for new challenges led him to make another dramatic career move. When his three-year contract with Def Jam expired at the end of 2007, he stepped down as president of the label. He explained that this decision was prompted in part by his rekindled enthusiasm for making new music. But he also wanted to pursue new business opportunities within the music industry that moved beyond the traditional framework of record labels. "The record business is in trouble, not the music business," he stated. "People are always gonna make music. But the record business, they've got some things to fix."[70]

In early 2008 Jay-Z made a deal with the concert promoter Live Nation worth an estimated $150 million. In addition to organizing, promoting, and selling tickets to live shows by Jay-Z, Live Nation also planned to distribute his albums, market his merchandise, and handle other aspects of his career. Jay-Z felt that Live Nation's consolidated approach gave it many different ways to reach consumers and keep up with rapid changes in the music industry. "Everyone's trying to figure it out," he said. "I want to be on the front lines in that fight."[71]

Jay-Z returned to his performance roots when he sang with Mary J. Blige during the Heart of the City tour at Madison Square Garden in 2008.

Most importantly for Jay-Z, the Live Nation deal included financing that allowed him to create his own entertainment venture, Roc Nation. One of Jay-Z's first priorities for Roc Nation was to form a new record label. He joined forces with two Norwegian entrepreneurs—Tor Erik Hermansen and Mikkel S. Eriksen, who owned a music production company called Stargate—to create StarRoc. Jay-Z's role with the new label was similar to the role he played at Def Jam: finding and promoting new talent.

Outside of the music industry, Jay-Z took a leading role in bringing a National Basketball Association (NBA) franchise to Brooklyn. After he became part owner of the New Jersey Nets

Showing His Versatility

Even as the popularity of hip-hop exploded around the world, some corners of the music scene remained steadfastly anti-rap. Jay-Z received a clear reminder of this attitude in February 2008, when he agreed to headline the famous Glastonbury Festival in England. First organized in the 1970s, the annual performing arts event featured live music by rock, folk, and alternative artists, as well as dance, comedy, and theatrical performances.

Jay-Z was the most prominent hip-hop artist ever invited to Glastonbury. His invitation created controversy as soon as the organizers announced it. Noel Gallagher, lead singer of the alternative-rock band Oasis, criticized the festival organizers for including Jay-Z among the headliners. "I'm sorry, but Jay-Z? No chance. Glastonbury has a tradition of guitar music," he declared. "I'm not having hip hop at Glastonbury. It's wrong."

Although some festival organizers and ticketholders agreed with Gallagher, many others spoke up on behalf of Jay-Z. His supporters argued that hip-hop was a legitimate musical genre that deserved to be showcased at Glastonbury. They noted that Jay-Z was an international superstar who could increase the festival's appeal for young audiences.

When the festival finally took place, Jay-Z made a dramatic musical response to the criticism. He appeared on stage accompanied by two acoustic guitar players and led the crowd in a rousing version of Oasis's biggest hit song, "Wonderwall." "Jay-Z took the Oasis star's criticism and turned it into one of the great Glastonbury moments," wrote one reviewer. "It was a moment that will surely go down in festival folklore."

Sources: Quoted in Colin Paterson, "Hip-Hop 'Wrong' for Glastonbury," *BBC News*, April 14, 2008. Available online at http://news.bbc.co.uk/1/hi/entertainment/7345780.stm. Quoted in "A Glastonbury Legend Is Born," *The Independent*, June 29, 2008. Available online at http://www.independent.co.uk/arts-entertainment/music/news/a-glastonbury-legend-is-born-856654.html.

in 2004, he helped negotiate a deal to move the team to a new stadium in New York City in 2011. He believed that having an NBA team would bring jobs, money, hope, and pride to Brooklyn.

"For a kid growing up in the Marcy Projects to be involved with a professional basketball team is way beyond anyone's dream," he declared. "You may think you can make it to the NBA, and that's a lofty dream. You never have the dream that you're gonna own the team."[72]

Gives Something Back

As he branched out into new areas of business, Jay-Z decided to sell his successful Rocawear clothing line to Iconix for $200 million. The deal increased the rap star's net worth to an estimated $555 million. Recalling his humble beginnings, Jay-Z felt a keen

Jay-Z visits with girls from a school in South Africa as part of his Water for Life world tour to help raise awareness about the global water crisis.

responsibility to use some of his enormous wealth to help others. "We're the first generation of hip-hop guys to really make the big money," he acknowledged. "The generation before us never made this type of cash, so it's on us to keep it going and give it back."[73]

Longing to have a positive impact on the world, Jay-Z actively supported a number of charitable causes. He spearheaded an annual toy drive, for instance, to ensure that all the poor kids in the Marcy Projects received gifts for Christmas. He also donated time and money to help people affected by the terrorist attacks of September 11, 2001, and people left homeless by Hurricane Katrina in 2005.

Jay-Z also became involved in efforts to address the global water crisis through MTV's Water for Life program. To help raise awareness of the cause, he appeared in a video for MTV, gave a series of interviews, and spoke at the United Nations. In all of these public appearances, Jay-Z cited statistics showing that 1.1 billion people around the world lacked access to safe drinking water. "As I started looking around and looking at ways that I could become helpful, it started at the first thing—water, something as simple as water," he said at a news conference. "It took very little, very little to see these numbers."[74]

In 2006 Jay-Z traveled to Africa, where he visited poor villages that suffered from severe water shortages. He felt honored to provide pumps that supplied the residents with clean water. "I've given money and written checks," he noted, "but when you're on the ground and you turn on the faucet and the village gets water for the first time, it's like nothing else."[75]

Jay-Z also felt a responsibility to be a positive role model for his young fans. He often visited schools and encouraged the students to believe in themselves and reach for their dreams. But Jay-Z always told his young audiences that his own path to success was not a realistic one for them to follow. Instead, he emphasized the importance of staying in school and getting a good education. "I wanted to set them straight on the likelihood of making it," he explained. "I broke it down to them by saying that they even had a better chance of being an NBA player than they did a rapper. I was like, 'Keep it real—there are about 200 or more NBA players getting a check. There are only about 10 to 20 rappers that are in the game making money with album after album. Do the math and get your education.'"[76] Jay-Z even established scholarship programs to help poor kids from the inner city attend college.

Campaigns for Obama

As part of his effort to make an impact on the world, Jay-Z became a high-profile supporter of Senator Barack Obama during the 2008 presidential election campaign. He held free concerts to

Jay-Z's Lady

On April 4, 2008, Jay-Z confirmed the suspicions of his longtime fans by marrying R&B sensation Beyoncé Knowles. Although the two stars were often seen together in public—fueling persistent rumors that they were dating—they kept the nature of their relationship strictly private.

Beyoncé was born on September 4, 1981. She became famous as the lead singer and creative force behind Destiny's Child, the most successful all-female musical group in history. Beyoncé launched her solo career in 2003 with the album *Dangerously in Love*, which featured two chart-topping singles and won five Grammy Awards. She built upon her successful recording career to become a model, actress, fashion designer, and record producer.

Jay-Z and Beyoncé worked together several times over the years. He supplied vocals on her hit songs "Crazy in Love" and "Déjà vu," while she made guest appearances on his songs "'03 Bonnie and Clyde" and "Hollywood." Still, they never confirmed any romantic involvement until they were married in a private ceremony, attended by forty friends and family members, at Jay-Z's penthouse apartment in New York City. Although the two stars never issued an official wedding announcement, the rumors were confirmed when Mary J. Blige offered her congratulations to Jay-Z on stage during a joint concert appearance the following night.

Jay-Z held free concerts and spoke at rallies to show his support for Barack Obama and encourage people to vote.

encourage people to register to vote, spoke at rallies, and went on a tour of swing states with the candidate. He described the historic significance of Obama's quest to become the first African American president of the United States at a campaign appearance in Philadelphia: "Rosa Parks sat so Martin Luther King could walk. Martin Luther King walked so Obama could run. Obama's running so we all can fly."[77]

At one campaign rally, Obama made a famous reference to the Jay-Z song "Dirt Off Your Shoulder." The candidate responded to criticism from Senator Hillary Clinton—his main rival for the Democratic nomination—with a gesture of brushing it off his shoulder. Columnist Maureen Dowd remarked that "it had to be the first time in history that a presidential candidate had a hip-hop moment."[78]

Jay-Z was thrilled when Obama won the presidency. "The joy, the incredible sense of pride… and the sense of hope it gave everybody in America that we're all now included in the American dream was priceless," he declared. "Now there's no excuses for anybody. Now you can look into any child's eyes and say, 'Keep it together, and you can be president.' It's not an easy thing, but it can happen, and we have evidence to the fact."[79]

Reaches the Penthouse

By the time he threw his considerable influence behind the Obama campaign, Jay-Z had sold more than thirty million records, earned four Grammy Awards, launched his own record labels and clothing lines, discovered and promoted several popular new recording artists, and become a powerful business executive. Jay-Z also purchased a $10 million, 13,000-square-foot, luxury penthouse apartment at the Time Warner Center near Central Park. On April 4, 2008, the apartment served as the setting for a wedding ceremony when Jay-Z married his longtime girlfriend, the phenomenally successful singer, model, and actress Beyoncé. To many longtime fans, the marriage seemed to be the culmination of an almost unbelievable rags-to-riches story.

And Jay-Z showed no signs of relinquishing his spot at the top of the music industry. Insiders routinely marvel that one of the most impressive things about Jay-Z has been his staying power.

In April 2008 Jay-Z married his longtime girlfriend, singer and actress Beyoncé Knowles.

Unlike many previous rap stars, he has remained tremendously popular for many years. "We've seen rappers killed, or just fall off," said Island Def Jam chairman Antonio "L.A." Reid. "Now we're watching the biggest rapper remain the biggest rapper. We've never seen this movie before."[80] Jay-Z added to his amazing string of top-selling albums with a third installment in the *Blueprint* series, which was released in September 2009. "I like the challenge of making great music and putting it out," he stated. "You have to make it for yourself, but of course you want people to appreciate it. I'm not immune to that."[81] *The Blueprint 3* soared to number one on the *Billboard* 200 and sold 476,000 in the first week.

Given his many accomplishments and his lasting influence on hip-hop culture, it is little wonder that numerous sources have referred to Jay-Z as the greatest MC of all time. Jay-Z declined to compare himself to top artists of the past, but he expressed determination to be the best that he could possibly be. "I can't get into that argument," he says, "because the people at the top of the game are no longer here with us. Big [the Notorious B.I.G.] and 'Pac [Tupac Shakur] didn't really get a chance to grow as artists. We never got to see where it woulda went. But I always felt that's what I was comin' to do, to be the best. I wasn't comin' in the game to be nothin' less."[82]

Notes

Introduction: Rising from the Lobby to the Penthouse

1. Toure, "Jay-Z: *The Black Album*," *Rolling Stone,* November 13, 2003. http://www.rollingstone.com/reviews/album/294305/review/6067977/theblackalbum.
2. Quoted in Josh Tyrangiel, "In His Next Lifetime," *Time,* November 24, 2003, p. 66.
3. Jake Brown, *Jay-Z...and the Roc-A-Fella Records Dynasty.* Phoenix, AZ: Colossus Books, 2005, p. xv.
4. Russell Simmons, "Jay-Z: Building the Hip-Hop Nation," *Time,* April 18, 2005, p. 75.

Chapter 1: Growing Up in the Ghetto

5. Quoted in Toure, "People of the Year 2001: Jay-Z, Hip-Hop's Number One Hustler," *Rolling Stone,* December 6, 2001, p. 131.
6. David Kohn, "The King of Rap," *60 Minutes,* August 13, 2003. http://www.cbsnews.com/stories/2002/11/18/60II/main529811.shtml.
7. Quoted in Rob Brunner, "Cash of the Titans," *Entertainment Weekly,* May 30, 2003, p. 26.
8. Quoted in Emma Forrest, "Jay-Z: Hip-Hop's Hottest Guy Talks about It All," *Teen People,* June 16, 2002, p. 54.
9. Quoted in Toure, "People of the Year 2001," p. 131.
10. Quoted in Lorraine Ali, "The Coolest Mogul," *Newsweek,* December 4, 2006, p. 63.
11. Quoted in Toure, "People of the Year 2001," p. 131.
12. Quoted in Toure, "The Book of Jay," *Rolling Stone,* December 15, 2005, p. 80. http://www.rollingstone.com/news/coverstory/book_of_jay-z.
13. Quoted in Toure, "The Book of Jay," p. 80.
14. Quoted in Kohn, "The King of Rap."
15. Quoted in Kohn, "The King of Rap."
16. Quoted in Forrest, "Jay-Z," p. 54.

17. Quoted in Toure, "The Book of Jay," p. 80.
18. Quoted in Toure, "The Book of Jay," p. 80.
19. Steve Huey, "Reasonable Doubt," AllMusic.com. http://www.allmusic.com/cg/amg.dll?p=amg&sql=10: hzfpxqthldje~T1.
20. Quoted in "Jay-Z: The Empire Strikes Back," *Vibe* (cover story), December 2000.

Chapter 2: Hitting It Big in Rap Music

21. Quoted in Simon Vozick-Levinson, "The Real Return of the King," *Entertainment Weekly,* November 2, 2007, p. 36.
22. Quoted in an interview for "CenterStage with Michael Kay," *YES Network,* March 4, 2008.
23. Quoted in Nick Charles and Cynthia Wang, "Street Singer: Jay-Z Makes the Switch from Hustler to Rap Star Look E-Z," *People Weekly,* April 5, 1999, p. 61.
24. Steven Thomas Erlewine, "Hard Knock Life, Volume 2: Jay-Z," *AllMusic.com*. http://www.allmusic.com/cg/amg .dll?p=amg&sql=10:jg3gtq9zmu46.
25. Quoted in Brunner, "Cash of the Titans," p. 26.
26. Quoted in Brunner, "Cash of the Titans," p. 26.
27. Quoted in Forrest, "Jay-Z," p. 54.
28. Kris Ex, "Vol. 3: Life and Times of S. Carter," *RollingStone .com.* http://www.rollingstone.com/artists/jayz/albums/ album/209448/review.
29. Quoted in Steve Jones, "Amid Hard Knocks, the Real Deal: Back for Another Round, Jay-Z Pulls No Punches," *USA Today,* December 27, 1999, p. D1.
30. Quoted in Lauren DeCarlo, "Jay-Z Goes on the Record," *WWD,* September 15, 2005, p. 20.
31. Quoted in Brunner, "Cash of the Titans," p. 26.
32. Quoted in Forrest, "Jay-Z," p. 54.
33. Quoted in Tyrangiel, "In His Next Lifetime," p. 66.

Chapter 3: Retiring as a Rap Artist

34. Jason Birchmeier, review of *The Blueprint, All Music Guide,* April 4, 2004. http://www.allmusic.com/cg/amg .dll?p=amg&sql=10:wxfrxq80ldde.

35. Neil Strauss, "The Blueprint: Jay-Z," *Rolling Stone,* October 2, 2001. http://www.rollingstone.com/reviews/album/216039/review/6067649/the_blueprint.
36. Quoted in Toure, "People of the Year 2001," p. 131.
37. Christian Hoard, "The Blueprint 2: The Gift and the Curse," *Rolling Stone,* November 12, 2002. http://www.rollingstone.com/reviews/album/255668/review/5943959?utm_source=Rhapsody&utm_medium=CDreview.
38. Quoted in Tyrangiel, "In His Next Lifetime," p. 66.
39. Quoted in Tyrangiel, "In His Next Lifetime," p. 66.
40. Toure, "Jay-Z: *The Black Album.*"
41. Quoted in Julian Roman, "Fade to Black: An Interview with Jay-Z," *Latino Review.* http://www.latinoreview.com/films_2004/paramountclassics/fadetoblack/jayz-interview.html.
42. Quoted in Steve Jones, "The Show Goes On for Jay-Z," *USA Today,* November 5, 2004, p. E12.

Chapter 4: Becoming a Business Mogul

43. Jeff Leeds and Lola Ogunnaike, "'Retired' Rapper Finds a Job atop Def Jam," *New York Times,* December 9, 2004, p. C1.
44. Quoted in Allison Samuels, "The Reign of Jay-Z," *Newsweek,* November 22, 2004, p. 66.
45. Quoted in Samuels, "The Reign of Jay-Z," p. 66.
46. Quoted in Samuels, "The Reign of Jay-Z," p. 66.
47. Quoted in Samuels, "The Reign of Jay-Z," p. 66.
48. Quoted in Jones, "The Show Goes on for Jay-Z," p. E12.
49. Quoted in Nadira A. Hira, "America's Hippest CEO," *Fortune,* October 17, 2005, p. 110.
50. Quoted in Tamara Conniff, "Jay-Z Named President, CEO of Def Jam Records," *Billboard,* December 8, 2004. http://www.billboard.com/bbcom/esearch/article_display.jsp?vnu_content_id=1000733930.
51. Quoted in Toure, "The Book of Jay," p. 80.
52. Quoted in Ali, "The Coolest Mogul," p. 63.
53. Quoted in Samuels, "The Reign of Jay-Z," p. 66.
54. Quoted in Leeds and Ogunnaike, "'Retired' Rapper Finds a Job atop Def Jam," p. C1.

55. Quoted in Toure, "The Book of Jay," p. 80.
56. Quoted in Steve Jones, "Jay-Z Is a Very Busy Man," *USA Today,* November 21, 2006, p. D5.
57. Quoted in Hira, "America's Hippest CEO," p. 110.
58. Hira, "America's Hippest CEO," p. 110.
59. Quoted in Jones, "Jay-Z Is a Very Busy Man," p. D5.
60. Quoted in Ali, The Coolest Mogul," p. 63.

Chapter 5: Having It All

61. Quoted in Clark Collis, "Jay-Z Returns," *Entertainment Weekly.com.* http://www.ew.com/ew/article/0,15345501,00.html?print.
62. Quoted in Vozick-Levinson, "The Real Return of the King," p. 36.
63. Rob Sheffield, "*American Gangster,*" *Rolling Stone,* November 15, 2007. http://www.rollingstone.com/artists/jayz/albums/album/17121991/review/17139179/american_gangster.
64. Quoted in Steve Jones, "For Jay-Z, *Gangster* Is the Soundtrack of His Life," *USA Today,* November 6, 2007, p. D1.
65. Quoted in Steve Jones, "Album, Film Round Out Jay-Z's *Gangster* Story," *USA Today,* November 6, 2007, p. D6.
66. Vozick-Levinson, "The Real Return of the King," p. 36.
67. Quoted in Jones, "For Jay-Z, *Gangster* Is the Soundtrack of His Life," p. D1.
68. Sheffield, "*American Gangster.*"
69. Quoted in Elliott Wilson, "The Audacity of Hov," *Vibe Online,* August 21, 2008. http://www.vibe.com/news/cover_stories/2008/08/jayz_cover/.
70. Quoted in Brunner, "Cash of the Titans," p. 26.
71. Quoted in Jeff Leeds, "In Rapper's $150 Million Deal, New Model for Ailing Business," *New York Times,* April 3, 2008, p. A1.
72. Collis, "Jay-Z Returns."
73. Quoted in Samuels, "The Reign of Jay-Z," p. 66.
74. Quoted in "Jay-Z Helps UN Focus on Water Crisis," *USA Today,* August 9, 2006. http://www.usatoday.com/life/people/2006-08-09-jay-z-water_x.htm.

75. Quoted in Ali, "The Coolest Mogul," p. 63.
76. Quoted in Samuels, "The Reign of Jay-Z," p. 66.
77. Quoted in Dan Martin, "Jay-Z: Obama's Running So We All Can Fly," *The Guardian,* November 5, 2008. http://www.guardian.co.uk/music/2008/nov/05/jayz-falloutboy.
78. Maureen Dowd, "Brush It Off," *New York Times,* April 20, 2008, p. L11.
79. Quoted in "Jay-Z on the Eve of the Inauguration," *MTV News Raw,* January 20, 2009. http://www.mtv.com/videos/news/333259/why-jay-z-backed-barack.jhtml#id=1603050.
80. Quoted in Ali, "The Coolest Mogul," p. 63.
81. Quoted in Vozick-Levinson, "The Real Return of the King," p. 36.
82. Quoted in Toure, "People of the Year 2001," p. 31.

Important Dates

1969
Jay-Z is born as Shawn Corey Carter on December 4 in Brooklyn, New York.

1981
His father, Adnes Reeves, deserts the family. A short time later, Jay-Z begins hustling drugs on the streets.

1989
Jay-Z contributes vocals to "Hawaiian Sophie" by Jaz-O. The song becomes a minor hit, and Jay-Z gains recognition as a talented young rapper.

1996
With partners Damon Dash and Kareem "Biggs" Burke, Jay-Z forms Roc-A-Fella Records and releases his first album, *Reasonable Doubt*.

1997
Roc-A-Fella signs a joint venture agreement with Def Jam Records. Jay-Z releases a second album, *In My Lifetime: Volume 1*.

1998
Jay-Z becomes a star with the release of his hugely successful third album, *Volume 2: Hard Knock Life*.

1999
Following the release of *Volume 3: Life and Times of S. Carter*, Jay-Z is arrested and charged with assault in connection with the stabbing of Lance "Un" Rivera at a New York nightclub.

2001
Jay-Z releases his critically acclaimed album *The Blueprint*.

2002

Jay-Z releases *The Blueprint 2*.

2003

Jay-Z announces his intention to retire as a recording artist to concentrate on business interests. He releases *The Black Album* and holds a farewell concert at Madison Square Garden.

2005

Jay-Z accepts a job as president and CEO of Def Jam Records.

2006

Jay-Z ends his retirement and returns to recording with the album *Kingdom Come*.

2007

Inspired by the film of the same name, Jay-Z records the concept album *American Gangster*. He steps down as president of Def Jam.

2008

Jay-Z marries his longtime girlfriend, Beyoncé, signs a $150 million deal with concert promoter Live Nation, and supports Barack Obama's presidential campaign.

For More Information

Books

Dennis Abrams, *Hip-Hop Stars: Jay-Z*. New York: Checkmark Books, 2008. Written for young readers, this biography provides a readable account of Jay-Z's life and work.

John Bankston, *Jay-Z: Hip-Hop Superstar.* Hockessin, DE: Mitchell Lane, 2004. This biography for young readers offers an overview of Jay-Z's contributions to hip-hop culture.

Geoff Barnes, *Hip-Hop: Jay-Z*. Broomall, PA: Mason Crest, 2008. This biography provides students with an in-depth look at Jay-Z's formative experiences and artistic and business successes.

Jake Brown, *Jay-Z...and the Roc-A-Fella Records Dynasty.* Phoenix, AZ: Colossus Books, 2005. Full of stories and quotes from Jay-Z, this book offers extensive background on his youth and early career.

Stacy Gueraseva, *Def Jam, Inc.: Russell Simmons, Rick Rubin, and the Extraordinary Story of the World's Most Influential Hip-Hop Label.* New York: One World/Ballantine, 2005. By probing the history of Def Jam, this book provides insight into the growth and influence of hip-hop culture.

Periodicals

Nadira A. Hira, "America's Hippest CEO," *Fortune,* October 17, 2005, p. 110. This lengthy feature includes biographical background information as well as quotations from interviews with Jay-Z.

Austin Scaggs, "Jay-Z," *Rolling Stone,* November 29, 2007, p. 55. In this wide-ranging interview, Jay-Z discusses his journey from the streets of Brooklyn to the presidency of Def Jam Records.

Toure, "The Book of Jay," *Rolling Stone,* December 5, 2005, p. 80. This *Rolling Stone* cover story focuses on Jay-Z's job as president and CEO of Def Jam Records.

Web Sites

Jay-Z (www.jayzonline.com). This rap-focused site offers the latest Jay-Z news and photos, plus lyrics to all of his songs.

Roc-A-Fella Records (www.rocafella.com). The official site of the record label includes a biography, news articles, photos, audio and video clips, tour dates, and other information about Jay-Z.

Rolling Stone (http://www.rollingstone.com/artists/jayz). The music magazine's Web site features a biography, discography, album reviews, and full text of archived articles about Jay-Z.

Index

A
Aaliyah, 13
Abandonment by father, 14
"Ain't No Nigga (Like the One I Got)" (song), 23–24
Albums
  American Gangster, 69–70
  The Black Album, 49–51
  The Blueprint, 43–46
  The Blueprint 2: The Gift and the Curse, 46–47
  Collision Course, 55–56
  Dynasty—Roc La Familia, 41, 43
  Kingdom Come, 67–68
  In My Lifetime: Volume 1 (album), 28–29
  Reasonable Doubt, 21–24
  Unfinished Business, 56–57
  Volume 2: Hard Knock Life, 29–31
  Volume 3: The Life and Times of S. Carter, 33, 35
American Gangster (album), 69–70
American Gangster (film), 68–69
Annie (musical), 30
Arrest, 38, 39
Attitude, 12–13, 63
Austin, Tony, 58

B
Backstage (documentary), 31
Basketball, 71–73
Battle-rap, 45–46
The Beatles, 50, 69
Bedford-Stuyvesant neighborhood, 11–13
Best of Both Worlds Tour, 56–57
Beyoncé. *See* Knowles, Beyoncé
Big Jaz. *See* Jaz-O
"Big Pimpin'" (song), 33, 35
Biggie Smalls. *See* Notorious B.I.G.
Billboard magazine standings
  American Gangster, 69
  The Blueprint, 44
  Dynasty—Roc La Familia, 43
  Reasonable Doubt (album), 21
  Volume 2: Hard Knock Life, 31
  Volume 3: The Life and Times of S. Carter, 43
Birchmeier, Jason, 44
The Black Album, 49–51
Bleek, Memphis, 26, 31
Blige, Mary J., 24, 51, 57, 71
The Blueprint (album), 43–46
The Blueprint 2: The Gift and the Curse (album), 46–47
Brooklyn, New York, 11–13, *12*, 15–17
Brown, Foxy, 23, 31, 51
Burke, Kareem "Biggs," 21, 22, 23
Business
  concert promotion, 70–71
  Def Jam Records, 58–64
  40/40 Club, 48
  National Basketball League team ownership, 71–73
  record company management, 57
  Roc-A-Fella Records founding, 21
  Rocawear, sale of, 73
  success, 8–10, 47–48
Busta Rhymes, 13

C
Campaigning, political, 75–77
Carter, Eric, 15
Carter, Gloria, 11, 14, 49
Chappelle, Dave, 13
Charity work, 73–75
Childhood, 11–13
   music and, 13–14
   See also Teenage years
Civil lawsuit, 39
Clothing line, 35–37
Collaboration
   Blige, Mary J., 24, 51, 57, 71
   Combs, Sean "Puffy," 27–28
   Fade to Black concert, 51–52
   Jaz-O, 18, 20
   Kelly, R., 56–57
   Knowles, Beyoncé, 54–55
   Linkin Park, 55–56
   Too $hort, 29
   Volume 2: Hard Knock Life, 31
Collision Course (album), 55–56
Combs, Sean "Puffy," 27, *28*, 69
Comeback album, 67–68
Concerts
   Best of Both Worlds Tour, *56,* 56–57
   farewell concert, 51–53, *52*
   for Barack Obama campaign, 75–76
   Hard Knock Life tour, 31
   Live Nation, 70–71
   Powerhouse concert, 65–66
Conservative groups, 31, 33
Controversies
   "Ain't No Nigga (Like the One I Got)" (song), 23–24
   "Big Pimpin'", 33, 35
   Volume 2: Hard Knock Life, 31, 33
Crack cocaine dealing, 15–17, *16*

"Crazy in Love" (song), 54–55
Creative control, 21
Crowe, Russell, 69

D
Danger Mouse, 50
Dash, Damon, 21, 22, 23
Debut album, 21–24
Def Jam Records
   business success, 8
   presidency, *58,* 58–64, 70
   Roc-A-Fella Records, joint venture with, 25–26, 59
"Dirt Off Your Shoulder" (song), 51, 77
Distribution deals, 21
DJs, 18, 34
DMX, *30*, 31
Documentaries
   Backstage, 31
   Fade to Black, 52–53
Dropping out of school, 20
Drug dealing, 15–17, 20
Dupri, Jermaine, 31
Dynasty—Roc La Familia (album), 41, 43

E
East Coast/West Coast feud, 26–27, 29
Elliott, Missy, 51
EMI, 50
Endorsements, product, 48
Eriksen, Mikkel S., 71
"Ether" (song), 46
Evans, Faith, 27

F
Fabolous, 13
Fade to Black concert, 51–53, *52*
Fade to Black (documentary film), 52–53
Fame, 41, 46–47

Index **91**

Fans, 24, 33, 66
Farewell album, 49, 51
Farewell concert, 51–53, *52*
Father, 11, 14, 49
Films
   American Gangster, 68–69
   Backstage, 31
   Fade to Black, 52–53
   Rock-A-Fella productions, 37
   Streets Is Watching, 37
40/40 Club, 48, *48*

G
Gallagher, Noel, 72
Ghostface Killah, 51
Glastonbury Festival, 72
Global water crisis, 73, 74
Gold records, 21, *23*
Golden Note Award, 55, *55*
Grammy Awards
   American Gangster, 70
   The Black Album, 51
   "Crazy in Love," 54–55
   McCartney, Paul, Jay-Z's appearance with, 50
   "Numb/Encore," 55
   rap category, 34
   Volume 2: Hard Knock Life, 29
The Grey Album, 50

H
"Hard Knock Life" (song), 30
Hard Knock Life tour, *30*, 31
"Hawaiian Sophie" (song), 18, 20
Hermansen, Tor Erik, 71
Hip-hop
   change in culture, 63
   clothing line, 35–37
   East Coast/West Coast feud, 26–27, 29
   at Glastonbury Festival, 72
   history, 18, 34

legacy, 77–79
music mixing, 50
Nas/Jay-Z feud, 44–46
popularity of Jay-Z, 35
Huey, Steve, 22
Hurricane Katrina relief, 74

I
"I Just Wanna Love U (Give It 2 Me)" (song), 41, 43
Iconix, 73
"In My Lifetime" (song), 20
In My Lifetime: Volume 1 (album), 28–29

J
Ja Rule, 31
Jay-Z, 9, 32, 42, *43*, 68
Jaz-O, 18, 20, 21
Jazzy Jeff, 34
Joint ventures, 25–26, 59
Just Blaze, 31

K
Kane, Big Daddy, 20
Kelly, R., 51, 56, *56*–57
Kent, Clark, 20
Kid Capri, 31
Kingdom Come (album), 67–68
Kit Kat Klub, 37–39
Knowles, Beyoncé, 51, 54–55, 75, 77, 78
Kool Herc, 18

L
Lady Sovereign, 63
Lawsuit, 39
Lee, Spike, 13
Legacy, 8–10, 77–79
Lil' Kim, 13
Linkin Park, 55–56
Live Nation, 70–71

Ludacris, 63
Lyrics, 14, 23–24

M
Marcy Projects
  childhood, 11–13
  drug dealing, 15–17
  Streets Is Watching (film), 37
  toy drive, 74
Marriage, 77
Martin, Chris, 67
Mashups, 55–56
McCartney, Paul, 50, *50*
MCs, 18, 34
Methodman, *30*
Morris, Doug, 64
Mos Def, 13
Mother, 11, 14, 49
Movies. *See* Films
MTV, 74
Music critics. *See* Reviews
Music success. *See* Legacy

N
Nas, 44–46, *45*, 66
National Basketball Association (NBA), 71–73
New artists, 61, 62–63
New Jersey Nets, 71–73
New York rap scene, 45–46
Ne-Yo, 63, 65
Notorious B.I.G., 13, 18, *19*, 26, *26*, 27, 29
"Numb/Encore" (song), 55

O
Obama, Barack, 75–77, *76*

P
Personality, 12–13, 63
Politics, 75–77
Popularity, 77–79

Powerhouse concert, 65–66
Priority Records, 21
Product endorsements, 48
Public housing, 11–13

R
Rap. *See* Hip-hop
"Real Niggaz" (song), 29
Reasonable Doubt (album), 21–24
Record companies. *See* Def Jam Records; Roc-A-Fella Records
Redman, *30*
Reebok, 48
Reeves, Adnes, 11, 14, 49
Reid, Antonio, *58*, 60
Retirement, 54–57, 66–67
Reviews
  American Gangster, 70
  The Black Album, 51
  The Blueprint, 44
  The Blueprint 2: The Gift and the Curse, 47
  Kingdom Come, 67–68
  In My Lifetime: Volume 1 (album), 29
  Reasonable Doubt (album), 22–23
  Volume 2: Hard Knock Life, 31
  Volume 3: The Life and Times of S. Carter, 35
Rihanna, *61*, 63
Rivera, Lance "Un," 37–40
Roc Nation, 71
Roc-A-Fella Records
  Backstage (documentary), 31
  clothing line, 35–37
  Def Jam Records, joint venture with, 25–26, 59
  film production, 37
  founding, 21
Rocawear, 35–37, *36*, 47, 73

Rock, Chris, 13
Role model, 74
Rosenblum, Renee, 17
Rubin, Rick, 59
Run DMC, 35

S
School, 17, 18, 20
Semtex, 63
Shakur, Afeni, 52, *52*
Shakur, Tupac, 26, *26*, 27, 29
Shootings, 15, *15*, 26–27
Siegel, Beanie, 43, 51
Simmons, Russell, 10, *58*, 59
Smith, Will, 34
Snoop Dogg, 27
Sports bars, 47–48
StarRoc, 71
Stoute, Steve, 62
Street hustling, 8–9
Streets Is Watching (film), 37
Success. *See* Business; Legacy
Sugarhill Gang, 34, *34*
"Super Ugly" (song), 46

T
"Takeover" (song), 45–46
Teachers, 17
Teenage years
  abandonment by father, 14
  drug dealing, 15–17
  hip-hop, interest in, 18
Timbaland, 31
Too $hort, 29
Toy Drive, 74
Tyson, Mike, 13

U
Unfinished Business (album), 56–57
Universal Music Group (UMG), 58–64

Urban clothing, 35–37, *36*
Usher, 57

V
Violence
  brother's shooting, 15
  drug dealing, 17
  East Coast/West Coast feud, 26–27
  Rivera, Lance "Un," stabbing of, 37–40
Volume 2: Hard Knock Life (album), 29–31
Volume 3: The Life and Times of S. Carter (album), 33, 35

W
Wallace, Christopher. *See* Notorious B.I.G.
Wallace, Voletta, 52, *52*
Warner Music Group, 59–60
Washington, Denzel, 68–69
Water for Life program, *73*, 74
Wedding, 77
West, Kanye, 63, 65
Westinghouse Technical High School, 18
"Where Have You Been?" (song), 43
The White Album, 50
Whitney High School, 18
Wilkens, Lenny, 13
Williams, Pharrell, 51

Y
Young Jeezy, 63, 65

Picture Credits

Cover: John Shearer/Wire Image/Getty Images

AP Images, 9, 12, 28, 30, 32, 36, 38, 43, 45, 48, 55, 56, 58, 66, 76, 78

© AsiaPix/Alamy, 42

Bennett Raglin/WireImage/Getty Images, 61

© Chad Batka/Corbis, 71

Frank Micelotta/Getty Images, 22

© Frank Chmura/Alamy, 15

Janette Beckman/Redferns/Getty Images, 34

Kevin Mazur/WireImage for New York Post/Getty Images, 52

L. Cohen/WireImage for the The Recording Academy/Getty Images, 50

© Larry Ford/Corbis, 23

© Lucas Jackson/Reuters/Corbis, 68

© Mikhael Subotzky/Corbis, 73

© Mitchell Gerber/Corbis, 19

© Photos 12/Alamy, 26

© Steve Starr/Corbis, 16

About the Author

Laurie Collier Hillstrom has written several previous volumes in the People in the News series, including *Al Gore*, *Dale Earnhardt Jr.*, and *Kelly Clarkson*. She lives in Michigan with her husband, Kevin Hillstrom, and twin daughters, Allison and Lindsay.